Acting on Script

A Grant's Crossing Story
By Jamie Tremain
Book #3

Acting Off-Script

Grant's Crossing Series
Book #3
Copyright © 2022 by Jamie Tremain
FIRST EDITION
Published September 15, 2022

For more information, contact: jamietremainJT@yahoo.com
www.jamietremain.ca[1]
Cover Design by Jennifer Gibson
www.JenniferGibson.ca[2]

---

1. http://www.jamietremain.ca

2. http://www.JenniferGibson.ca

Acknowledgements

From Liz:

Thank you to our loyal readers and fans, who keep me motivated to have another story waiting to be told, whether for Dorothy Dennehy, Alysha Grant, or perhaps one day soon – a new character waiting to be introduced.

As always, support from my wonderful husband, and family, is never taken for granted!

From Pam:

Always grateful for reader support – it's for you we continue to write.

From Jamie Tremain:

We depend on the support system, and friendship, of our fellow Genre5 writers, and the invaluable feedback received from our Beta Readers – Gloria, Linda, Michele, and Wendy. Thanks for keeping us sharp!

CHAPTER ONE

Alysha

No need to wait for tomorrow's Gazette. News of a body recently discovered was all over town. According to rumours, a woman's body had been found beneath renovation materials at the old movie theatre on the main street. I'd driven by the place on my way home. A couple of police cars and the usual crowd of onlookers left no doubt something suspicious had happened.

As for me, I'd heard the news earlier when a client coming into Bennett Howes' real estate office had shared the revelation - with a little too much enjoyment in my opinion.

Cassie DeSouza, our cook at Leven Lodge, and never-ending information pipeline, had likely been more than happy to bring all the residents up to speed as well. In my mind's eye I could see her even now, putting her theories forth to anyone there who'd listen.

The workday for me had ended, and these thoughts were on my mind as I returned home. I sighed to myself, grateful to have avoided seeing anyone as I made my way up to the third floor of Leven Lodge.

First order of the day - shed my professional appearance and get comfy. Brush out the hair product which keeps my curls in line and find my yoga pants. Not that I do yoga - running's my thing. And I hoped to have time before dinner to manage at least a short run.

Sitting at my desk at the top of the renovated farmhouse meant being in my happy place. Although I had a town-based office as a realtor apprentice at Bennett Howes Real Estate brokerage, I preferred my spot overlooking the meadow where the alpacas we raised roamed all day. They never felt the cold and would enjoy the snow we'd see in the coming weeks.

Thinking of snow reminded me I'd need to get another pair of casual dress pants hemmed. I preferred shorts and dresses in the warmer weather but being in the business world meant I needed dressier wear for colder weather. I'd procrastinated having pants hemmed - the curse of being just over five feet. Pants were always too long!

Bennett was an extraordinary mentor and I appreciated all I'd learned from him over the past months. He hadn't earned the title of real estate king in Grant's Crossing for nothing. He's given me the confidence to strike out and start bringing in sales on my own. Earning commission meant extra funds at last for projects around Leven Lodge.

Not long after I started working with him, he'd met Nina Mikado, who is one of our temporary guests here. He'd fallen for her from the get-go, and it appeared they spent all their free time together. I hadn't intended to be a matchmaker!

Grant's Crossing had become a destination town for big-city folks. But there's the irony. They want to leave the city for that small-town feel, but then they end up pushing for the conveniences they're used to. Both Bennett and I are determined to have Grant's Crossing retain its friendly small-town atmosphere. Finding the balance will be a challenge.

The upside? Houses were moving quickly, and demand threatened to outstrip supply. More than one developer had approached town officials for zoning permits.

The Rivermill Resort and Spa was a recent commercial addition and had quickly become a favourite for out-of-town visitors. Or maybe it was the notoriety around it due to a murder on the grounds back in the summer which made it popular?

Murder! That brought me back to the news today, and of course, to events earlier this year, when one of our residents, Dianne Mitchell, had come under suspicion. Leven Lodge, which I own and operate, is home to several interesting, retired folks. Dianne is not only a resident but has become a friend and we were all grateful when she'd been cleared of any implication in the murder, despite the fact her fiery temperament had the cops wondering if she'd been involved with the murder of a former lover, Sloane Jackson.

I admired her fashion sense and even though she lived with residents older than her, she's not ready to give up her hairstylist, or cut back on her make-up budget. I'm working on my confidence level and could do worse than follow her example.

A couple of bills had arrived in the mail, and I put them to one side. My mind rested again on the latest town news, and I truly hoped this murder would have no connection to Leven Lodge or anyone who lived here! We'd had more than our fair share in the short time I'd been here.

Dinner would be served soon, and I predicted lively comments about the death. My boyfriend, Jeff Iverson, needed to get cleaned up before dinner. He spent most of his days with the alpacas I mentioned.

A knock at the door brought me to my feet. I barely had the door open before Dianne strode in, holding an ice pack to her face. "Can I have a word before dinner?"

CHAPTER TWO

Dianne

I stood behind the two old biddies in Grant's Crossing Food Market and did a slow burn. People could be so ignorant, and age is no excuse.

Their white heads leaned together, each trying to outdo the other with their gossip and judgy comments. Marjorie Bell and Janice O'Hare were apparently experts on the newest residents of Leven Lodge.

"And you'd think after they've lived in this country, they'd wear normal clothes," said Marjorie. To which Janice replied, with an Irish lilt, "Government's letting too many immigrants in."

Double standards; still alive and well.

They moved closer to the cashier and began putting items on the conveyor belt. If I recalled correctly, these two spinsters shared an apartment over one of the stores on the main street. I imagined them sitting for hours at a time, watching the street, and making comments about all who passed within their line of sight.

I knew they were referring to Sasitha and Bachan Patel, who had recently moved into Leven Lodge, the retirement home where I also lived. They'd raised a few eyebrows when they first arrived to be sure, but I enjoyed the change-up in our group dynamics and was happy to have them. Leven Lodge accommodated eight residents and we would be a full house again with the return of Minnie Parker - probably the most colourful and eccentric character I've ever met.

Minnie was elderly, and cranky. After a dramatic shift in her mental health, she'd been briefly hospitalised - about the same time I had been under suspicion of murder - and was expected back as early as tomorrow. To say we'd had an eventful summer would be an understatement!

But I've digressed. Back to my predicament.

The check-out girl ignored the nosy hags' snide comments as she processed their order. She was young and I hoped more tolerant of her world outlook than her customers. I glanced at the tongue-waggers' purchases. It made me grateful the lodge supplied a variety of meals for its residents. No fish fingers or frozen pizzas for us!

The red plastic divider went on the conveyor belt, and I began to place the few items I had. I faltered when I heard Marjorie's accusation. "Dollars to donuts, they had something to do with that body, too!"

Oh, brother – they'd pushed the wrong button. I tapped Marjorie on the shoulder. "Excuse me. You're personal friends with the Patels, are you?" Sarcasm would probably be lost on them, but I continued. "Saw one of them commit murder as well? Guess you should be talking to the police and not wasting everyone's time here!" And of course, my voice had risen like a thermometer the longer I talked. Not the first time I've had an audience.

I was gratified to see Marjorie's face turn a lovely beet red. The satisfaction was short-lived. Janice pulled her friend back and flew into my face quicker than lightning. "Mind your own business, Miss Mitchell. Marj has a right to her opinion." The spittle in the corner of her mouth was a nice touch and I backed up a step.

"Not when it affects the character of someone I know." The fire was lit, and I knew I should stop, but I didn't. "You know, Karma is a bitch and I hope she brings friends to everyone who gossips and spreads rumours. It's not so much fun when you're on the receiving end."

I saw it coming but couldn't move fast enough. The shove from Janice pushed me back into an unsteady display of canned tomatoes and down I went. Not small cans either. The extra-large size and two of them bounced off my face. The only sound I heard came from cans rolling on the tile floor in all directions.

Then it got noisy. A staff person helped me to my feet. A couple of shoppers applauded, but whether for me or the tittle-tattle twins I didn't know or much care. I needed to get out of there, my mind already calculating where I'd need to go for my shopping needs in the future.

Someone handed me a grocery bag with a hurried explanation. "They're paid for, but I think you should leave and get some ice on your face." Expressions on faces ranged from disbelief to smirks. I grabbed the bag and forced myself to exit with some dignity. Back in my car, I gingerly touched my cheekbone. The rear-view mirror was not kind.

I'd need to talk to Alysha first before news of this got to her ears.

CHAPTER THREE

Alysha

So much for my brief moment to enjoy the satisfaction of another successful house closing. I'd wanted to savour the accomplishment of one more credit to my growing real estate career. Whatever had happened to Dianne meant I wouldn't be going for a run with Jeff, either. I'd been this close to changing into my running gear! Interruptions went with the territory of owning a retirement home - especially when you lived there as well.

Jeff and I had taken on the operation of Leven Lodge together. We'd been living together since university, and he happily agreed to stay with me when I decided to take up the inheritance I'd been given. We were opposites in a lot of ways. Jeff's a computer nerd and knows his way around a barbecue grill. He's tall, and his sweet personality goes over well with the older ones - especially the ladies. Most of them were at least thirty years older than Jeff, so I didn't need to be jealous.

I tried not to sigh as visions of a head-clearing run in the cool autumn air dissolved. What the heck. Jeff wasn't here yet anyway. Still out in the fields or barn caring for the alpacas - not enough hours in the day for him when it comes to his pride and joy. Don't get me wrong, he also is responsible for other chores; yard work, minor maintenance and takes a run to the dump at least once a week. Some days I felt as if I needed to schedule time with him to make sure we saw each other.

"Alysha?"

"Oh, sorry. Lots on my mind. What on earth happened?"

"That's what I'm here to tell you. And I wanted to catch you before dinner." She strode further into the apartment, headed for the sofa and parked her butt.

She pulled the ice pack away from her face and I winced. "Ouch. Hope you've got ample make-up to match the bruises. Would a glass of wine help?" And then with some guilt at not asking first, I offered an apology by asking if she'd seen a doctor. She told me she wasn't going to bother.

Dianne smiled at me as she repositioned the ice pack against her face. "I've never heard you use sarcasm. But take it from me, not everyone will get it and it's not your style. Thanks for the offer, but I've taken some pain pills so I'd better pass. Raincheck?"

"Of course. Anytime. Now tell me how you earned the new look? And how's the other guy's face?"

She chuckled. "Oh, no, Alysha. I'm the only one sporting bruises. But there's a couple of people I know who could do with a bump or two!"

Dianne proceeded to tell me about her confrontation at the market regarding the Patels. I sensed she might be elaborating a bit on the shoving match resulting in her injuries, but that's Dianne. If what she told me was true, I might have said something in the store as well. She wasn't quite finished, and I let her vent.

"I can't understand the narrow-mindedness of some people. The Patels are a terrific couple and make a welcome addition to the Lodge and Grant's Crossing. I'm sorry, Alysha, those small-minded people upset me and it's no secret I have a motor mouth. I am more than a little embarrassed now, but I did want you to hear it from me, first." She stood. "Sorry, I know you're only just home from work and I've taken enough of your time."

"Not a problem, but as long as you're certain you don't need medical attention, I'll need to move you along. I appreciate you coming to me. Nothing worse than a blindside, so thanks." We moved toward the door, but I inwardly groaned when I heard footsteps approaching. Now what?

I opened the door, diverting another knock. The home's housekeeper, Jan Young, stood there.

Where would I be without Jan? Her stabilizing influence reached all corners of Leven Lodge. She's become a mother-figure to me and keeps me grounded.

Over the summer a few grey strands had made their mark in her beautiful long black hair. I envied her make-up free complexion. To me, she didn't resemble her age.

Her wide grin and sparkling brown eyes made me believe she had news. Uncharacteristic of her, she also seemed flustered. Her hands twisted at the apron around her waist.

"Alysha!" And then she noticed Dianne. "Oh my! What happened?" Without waiting for an answer, she circled back to the reason she'd come. Dianne's face came second to Jan's news. "You'll never guess. Minnie's here! The hospital released her a day early. She arrived by taxi, and I've taken her to her room. Thankfully, she had been accompanied by an aide. Someone's signals got crossed and I never received a phone call to let me know, but all the paperwork is in order."

She finally ran out of steam, and I could get a word in edgewise. "And how is she?"

"Better than I expected. She seems happy to be home and made no fuss. I guess we'll have to wait and see."

"Wow. So much for schedules, right? Are you okay? You said you had everything ready for her tomorrow, so... I'm glad she's back."

Jan nodded. "I think so, little one. But coming this late in the afternoon - I don't know if she'll want dinner." And then her eyes returned to Dianne.

"Jan, take a breather. I'll go and welcome Minnie back into the fold, you can let Dianne provide the war details. Stay up here for a bit, where no one can find you, I hope."

Jan straightened out her apron and went to Dianne. "My, what a bump. Okay, let's hear it, Dianne. But the condensed version please, I have to help Cassie with dinner."

I slipped out of the room, leaving Dianne and Jan to catch up. I ran down the stairs and tentatively knocked on Minnie's door.

I fixed a smile on my face to greet her, not sure what to expect. She'd been hospitalized after a breakdown in the summer. A long-time resident of the home, she had a contentious streak and didn't play well with others. But thanks to my grandmother, Estelle Grant, Minnie was forever promised a home with Leven Lodge.

She possessed a sharp tongue and spoke without a filter, but she was as much a part of our home as anyone. Her and her knitting. I wondered if she still knitted like a fiend.

When she had her breakdown, we learned her story. And came to understand some of her eccentricities. Hoarding had been the worst, with offensive odours from rotting food affecting Dianne the most. Their rooms shared a bathroom and a dank and offensive smell often pervaded Dianne's space and clung to Minnie herself.

All in the past now, the hoarding anyway, and I anxiously wondered what therapy had done for her over the weeks she'd been under care. While she'd been away all the residents voiced their concern for her.

So, I was astonished, to say the least when her door opened and the tiny birdlike woman - one of the few people I could look eye-to eye with - threw her arms around my neck.

"Oh, Alysha, it's so good to see you and thank you for having me back."

"Minnie, you look wonderful... and rested. Welcome home. The others will be happy to see you. Will you join us for dinner tonight?"

"I don't think so. Not tonight. I need to settle in and unpack. I bought some new clothes. Frank helped me pick them out. He's been marvellous to me."

It was like a different woman speaking. Minnie had always been thrifty with her words; she'd said more in the last few minutes than I'd ever heard. "I understand, of course. How about I have a tray brought up and you can eat while you unpack?"

"If it's no trouble? I will be down for breakfast."

"No trouble at all. The others will be so anxious to see you! And I'm happy to hear Frank has been helpful. He's been a loyal friend to you for a long time."

She nodded and lowered her eyes. Was she shy about mentioning Frank? They did have a history. Frank Adams, our part-time gardener and general handyman, had known Minnie for decades - they'd nearly married at one point. Age and arthritis slowed him a bit, but his help around the grounds, and with Minnie, was invaluable.

"If you change your mind, we'll be meeting in the front room in thirty minutes for the usual Happy Hour." Even though Minnie never drank alcohol, she loved our Happy Hours. There would usually be someone who made a target for one of her barbs.

"Not tonight, Alysha, but thank you. I'm nervous to see everyone again. Will they accept me back? And Dianne? How did she ever put up with me?"

"Minnie, take your time and only join us when you are comfortable. Oh, and we have some new guests I believe you will like. Did Frank mention them to you? The Patels. They're in the McTaggarts old room."

"Poor Jock and Bea. Seems a long time ago now."

At the risk of a sentimental slide into memories of those no longer with us, I changed gears. "So don't forget I'll have a tray brought up in a little bit. But if you need anything, let me, or Jan know. Okay?"

I moved away and wonder of wonders she smiled at me. I'll have a word with Frank - he'll probably be able to add a bit more information.

My watch said there'd be no run now. But I did hear Jeff greeting someone in the kitchen below. So, he'd finally torn himself away from the alpacas. If not before dinner, then afterwards, we needed to talk. Time for a re-adjustment, or a refocus of his time - on me!

CHAPTER FOUR

Dianne

The swelling had subsided, but I didn't have enough foundation, or skill, to disguise the dark bruises forming on my cheek. I had my story at the ready and rehearsed it again as I headed downstairs for breakfast.

A copy of the morning Gazette lay on a table in the front hallway. Of course, the body discovered yesterday warranted headline status. But there were scant details. Suspicious death, next of kin not yet notified, police investigating, and so on. The theatre undergoing renovations had been a hot topic of late around here. An established theatre group - The Countryside Players - had outgrown their small facility about twenty minutes away from Grant's Crossing and had recently bought the old movie theatre. They'd even scored a funding grant from the town council to help them establish their presence. Another future tourist draw. Some of our gang had already volunteered to take part in behind-the-scenes activities. Well, it would all be on hold for a while now, I guess.

Chattering voices and the enticing lure of fresh coffee said Leven Lodge's day had started. No one paid much attention as I poured myself a coffee from the side table and took my place. All eyes were on our returning Minnie Parker.

When I'd last seen the feisty senior, she had lost all her belligerence and fighting spirit. And boy, over the years, we had some lively matches. No one had been safe from her verbal attacks - except Frank. But one day this past summer it all came crashing down, literally, for her and led to a hospital stay. Today, she wore updated clothes and – wait – was that a smile on her face?

Any concerns I entertained about her reaction to the Patels were non-existent. Minnie sat next to Sasitha Patel, who couldn't do enough

16

for her – passing her the butter, filling her water glass. Her husband, Bachan, who was always pleasant, ensured his wife's plate was never empty. A little too much sweetness for me first thing in the morning. Quite the reverse to how our former residents, Jock and Bea McTaggart, behaved.

The Patels were an attractive couple, to say the least. In their late sixties, I'd heard, they didn't look their age. Bachan sported a greying and neatly trimmed beard, which contrasted so well against his dark skin. He retained a youthful vigour and build. The air of confidence he carried only added to his overall appeal. And Sasitha? A classic beauty, with her still jet-black hair. She usually wore it long, flowing over her shoulders. They both favoured colourful clothing and we'd been awed whenever Sasitha dressed in one of her exquisite sarees. The classic Nehru jackets which Bachan preferred suited him. Stunning. She was a little shorter than her husband, and her svelte figure put me to shame.

Rose Edwards raised a questioning eyebrow at me as I sat down, but her twin sister, Lily Courtemanche, hadn't even glanced my way. And Philip McGee, our retired university professor? I wouldn't expect a comment from him unless the place was on fire, or he'd misplaced his elbow-patched sweater.

Nina Mikado hadn't made it downstairs yet, and Alysha and Jeff had followed me in. Alysha unusually quiet, and Jeff wore a scowl. I noticed they greeted others but didn't say much to each other. At least Alysha spoke to me, in low tones.

"Morning, Dianne. Still tender?"

"A little, yes. But no one seems to have noticed. Minnie's taken the spotlight."

Alysha smiled. "No kidding. Hope you're not upset?"

"I'll survive. So, you talked with her last night. How is she?"

"I need to speak with Jan later about medications and follow-up appointments. But, overall, I'd say she's made a remarkable recovery. I feel like we have to get to know her all over again."

"Sasitha has taken a shine to her. Look."

Sasitha had clasped Minnie's hands in her own. "Oh, my dear new friend, Minnie. I am thinking we will be the best of friends. One hundred percent. What do you say?"

A year ago, Minnie would have never allowed such familiarity. And I could only imagine the reaction our Minnie of old would have had. Today, she offered a bashful smile to Sasitha. "I hope so, too. You know, I wasn't here when you arrived. What made you decide to come to Grant's Crossing?"

Sasitha's eyes sparkled, and she glanced around the table. "I am knowing everyone here has heard already our story. May I repeat for Minnie?"

No one disagreed and once Bachan refilled his wife's glass with more orange juice she began.

"My most lovely husband, Bachan and I, had an arranged marriage where we lived in Pune, India. We were young and that was the way. A very happy thing we liked each other." She giggled.

I never grew tired of the obvious affection Sasitha and Bachan had for each other. I stole a glance at Jeff and Alysha. She smiled, but a deep frown still creased his face.

Sasitha beamed at her husband. "Just as today, my husband has always been so handsome, and he became an actor! I was so proud. After some time, he found for me employment working on costume design for the movies as well. We met so many famous people! Later, dear Minnie, please come and see pictures I have of those days. You will enjoy."

I glanced over at the sisters. Twins in name only. In their early seventies, they were as different as night and day. Both in physicality and personality. Rose had the bored expression of someone who'd heard a story a million times, but Lily sat with her hands cupping her head and nothing could tear her gaze away from Sasitha. I didn't mind hearing it again. And Bachan? He never interrupted his wife and let her be the star when telling it. My cynical side said he likely knew better than to interrupt her, so she'd finish up already! But maybe not. They doted on each other.

I refocused on Sasitha. "And then in 1975, we decided to leave India for your beautiful Canada. We already had friends living in Scarborough so that is where we went, too. For many years we lived there."

Her smile dimmed, and I knew what was next. "In those years we had hopes for starting a family. To raise children and... But the gods determined no. Not one, but three children I miscarried. It was not to be." She raised her hand to wipe at moisture leaking from her eyes. Not a sound from the table other than the tinkle of her numerous wrist bracelets.

Minnie reached out a hand and touched Sasitha's arm. She, too, had suffered a miscarriage. She didn't say a word, but if there was ever a poster for bonding moments, they'd be featured on it.

Sasitha patted Minnie's hand and continued. "Many times, when we were not working, we liked to take drives out into the country. So many pretty small towns we found. Isn't that right, babu?"

"Exactly as you say, priya." Bachan's warm, brown eyes were tender as he spoke to his wife. "Many happy hours we spent on these trips."

"And so," Sasitha picked up the tale. "When it came time to imagine retiring, we decided to make one of these beautiful places our home. We drove through Grant's Crossing a year ago and knew we needed to be here."

Lily clapped her hands in joy. "I love this story, and I'm so happy you decided to come here to live."

Outbursts weren't common for Lily, and she reddened immediately and gave the last piece of toast on her plate serious consideration.

Philip had remained silent during the recounting, but I sensed his agitation to get away from the table. He has autism and while he's connected well with Jeff and Frank Adams, he prefers not to linger over meals or social gatherings. Books and alpacas are his escape.

Jan must have been waiting outside the dining room because as soon as Lily spoke, she entered and began clearing away the breakfast remains. Clearly, she'd given the Patels time to connect with Minnie and I gave her a smile of acknowledgement when our eyes met.

Still no sign of Nina. Not a surprise. Our spirited writer-in-residence wasn't a morning person. Her temporary stay for the summer had been extended to the end of the year. Not without some challenges. Her tiny mutt, Hemingway, being chief among them. When she'd shown an interest in developing a story, using the twins as role models, Rose and Lily had cajoled Jan and Alysha into extending her stay. To the surprise of some, Lily had a way with Hemingway and her promise to keep him out of Jan's prized gardens helped nudge Jan toward agreeing. In my humble opinion, her romance with Alysha's boss accounted for most of her absences.

Jan's entrance signalled the end of breakfast, although we were all free to hang around for as long as we wanted. Philip was the first to leave, with the twins not far behind.

And still, Jeff and Alysha had barely spoken. Jeff pushed his chair away. Alysha reached for his arm. "A run later?"

"Not sure," he mumbled and left.

The Patels stood, and Sasitha put a hand on Minnie's shoulder. "Please, come with us. We have much to talk about."

Minnie smiled up at her new friend. "Can I see some of those pictures you mentioned?" Then she turned to me. "Oh, and Dianne? I hope those bruises on your face aren't as painful as they look."

I was floored and had no response. Who was this person and what had happened to the Minnie of old? What a difference. Was it too good to be true? Guess I hadn't needed to have a story ready to explain the bumps and bruises after all. But the day wasn't over.

And then they were gone, leaving me with Alysha.

"Right. What's going on with you two?"

CHAPTER FIVE

Alysha

I'd have to delay this conversation. "Sorry, Dianne, I have a busy day ahead of me. Can we talk after supper this evening?"

She nodded. "Sounds like a plan. How about I see if Jan's available for one of our tete-a-tetes? I think we're overdue for one."

Jan, Dianne, and I had developed a routine of meeting on a semi-regular basis to catch up on Leven Lodge-related items. Dianne had earned our trust to be included, but I stayed on the alert to ward off any potential gossip. I counted Dianne as a true friend, even though she was old enough to be my mother, but her tendency toward hearsay and sarcasm needed watching. Otherwise, we three made a strong and united team.

"I'll leave it with you. Right now, I have to fly. Later."

True, I did have a busy day ahead of me and not much time to reflect on Dianne's question. What was going on with Jeff and me?

Knowing Dianne, she'll demand answers but I'd rather Jan's voice of reason than her jaded and often disparaging comments of men in general.

The sun shone in a cloudless, brilliant blue sky as I drove into town. Thanksgiving was behind us, and we now had a typical fall day. I pushed aside all thoughts of Dianne and Leven Lodge and planned my workday.

With two scheduled house showings, phone calls to make, and an overflowing email inbox, there'd be scant time to think about much else.

My morning had been going well. I now added the possibility of listing a new property in the next day or two, and I felt pumped. I'd just hung up the phone when the front door to the business swept open, and I heard, "There you are, chickie."

Like an elevator in freefall, my mood dropped. Nina Mikado's personality ran to extremes, and I couldn't even imagine why she'd come looking for me. Today's outfit may have been meant to represent beautiful autumn colours, but the exaggerated size of bright yellow and red maple leaves adorning her tunic top made me blink. I scanned for signs of her muse, Hemingway. She'd often wrap up her tiny dog in a sling disguised as a scarf. But not today; he was absent. Lily had become fond of the dog and never hesitated to dog-sit, so I assumed that was the case today.

"Something I can help you with, Nina?" I vowed to be all business.

She pranced across the room and sat in the chair on the other side of my desk. Her flowery scent drifted in behind her. "No, nothing important. I came into town for this and that, and thought I'd like to see where you work."

More likely hoping to see Bennett, I thought.

She scanned the small office that was mine, for now. "You could do with some plants or some art on the wall to liven this up."

"I may not be here for long, Nina. My goal is to have my own real estate office in the future. Your friend, Bennett, has kindly provided this space to help me get established."

"Did I hear my name, then?"

Oh, brother, this little office of mine wasn't big enough to hold these two gigantic egos. Bennett enjoyed legendary status in Grant's Crossing for his real estate success and his community involvement. I couldn't fault him on either count, but some days I felt he'd be better suited to an oil field in Texas. Stetson hat and all.

"Nina, you didn't tell me you'd be stopping by."

Was it just me, or did infatuated seniors seem unnatural?

She gushed. She actually gushed! "I thought I'd surprise you in hopes you might be able to enjoy a coffee break with little old me?"

I bit my lip watching the game unfold in front of me.

He beamed. "What could be better than a chance to spend time with you? We'll leave Alysha to her work, shall we?"

And just like that, they left.

***

Conversation at dinner centred around the recent death at the old cinema. Official police news was sparse, but it leaned toward a suspicious death.

Cassie DeSouza, our cook, and resident gossip couldn't wait to share, with any who'd listen, what she knew about this recent Grant's Crossing happening. She tended to be scatter-brained, but maybe it was her age. At twenty-two, her main responsibility around the lodge focused on meal prep - and experimenting with recipes. Aside from Jeff, she was closest in age to me, but our eight-year difference seemed worlds apart at times. During the week she lived on-site - sharing a small apartment with Jan, and most evenings and off-days found her helping out at the Crossings Tavern, owned by her father.

As she brought in a couple of pies and a bowl of whipped cream for our dessert, she chattered on a mile a minute. Her nervous energy must be what helped her stay so thin!

"And they're saying the body is April Lancashire. You know, the treasurer of Countryside Players. Probably no surprise. Not too many people liked her. She was bossy and wanted things her way. A couple of players were threatening to quit. Maybe one of them did it? And the place isn't even fixed up. More delays." She stacked up some of our empty plates and never skipped a beat. "Bet this means I won't be doing any catering for them yet."

"Slow down a minute, Cassie." I could see eager faces around the table wanting more news, but this was far from official, and I detested false information being spread. "How do you know all this?"

She turned, holding the heavy tray of dirty dishes. "It's all over the tavern, right? Lots of the actors come in. And I hear what they're saying."

"So, not from the police, but just speculation? Cassie?"

She shifted from foot to foot. "Sorry. Yes, you're right Alysha. But still…"

"How about you concentrate on clearing up?"

I wanted to add she should go puff on one of her joints to calm down a bit. This kind of hearsay wouldn't be healthy for the reputation of the town. And could affect real estate sales. Who'd want to move to a small town where murder seemed to breed?

The evening meal had pretty much finished, and people began to move out, but Dianne hung back.

"So, we're good to visit with Jan in about an hour. Okay?"

I gave her a thumbs-up. "See you there." And then I scooted out of the room.

I still wasn't sure how I'd answer Dianne's question from the morning. She'd noted the tension between Jeff and me. And if she'd picked up on it, Jan would as well.

It's not so much tension as his complete lack of interest in me, unless it involves alpacas. He's anxious to build up capital to increase the herd and cover the expenses involved. So, he should understand I'm biding my time to build business capital of my own. Surely, he can see the reason in my budgeting. But in my mind, coming second best to four-legged creatures, even though they're adorable, has left me feeling neglected.

A guilty thought niggled at me as I brushed through my unruly curls - perhaps I've been neglecting him over my career and responsibilities here? We'd have to clear the air. And soon. But I wouldn't have a chance now. Dianne would want to know what's going on. The timing for a chat with her and Jan couldn't be worse. Too late to avoid it now.

I ran down the stairs, skipping the elevator as usual. The house was quiet except for the twins watching Jeopardy in the media room. I did a double-take when I realized Minnie sat with them.

I tapped on the door to the rooms Jan and Cassie shared and was greeted with a hug and a warm embrace from Jan. "Come and sit down, little one."

Dianne, already there, seemed quite comfortable. The open bottle of wine in front of her I took to mean she'd done with her pain meds. By Jan sat a teapot.

Dianne and Jan were nothing alike, and despite the difference in all our ages, we bonded well - perhaps due in part to events of the past year or so. If I had to say why, maybe because Jan was a motherly figure, while Dianne could fill the role of a much older sister or favourite aunt. I enjoyed their company, but tonight, I found myself irritated with Dianne.

I felt defensive. Her question at breakfast would need answering. She patted the seat next to her and offered me a glass of wine. Needing the distraction as means to play for time, I accepted.

She started with small talk. "I hear Nina popped in for a visit today."

"For a few minutes, yes." The less said about that for now, the better.

"They make a pair," said Dianne with a chuckle. But then she got down to business.

"Alysha. I may have overstepped my bounds, but Jan and I were talking earlier today, and we're both concerned about you. I hope you don't mind. I told her I thought you were out of sorts because of a rift or something between you and Jeff?"

I put the wine glass down and forced myself to stay cool, but I was annoyed big time.

"To answer your question Dianne, I do mind you giving your interpretation of my love life to Jan. I'd rather keep my love life, private."

Dianne waded right in as if she hadn't heard. "But Alysha, we've noticed you two aren't communicating. And we can..."

Jan, who had been a silent onlooker, couldn't keep quiet a minute longer. "Dianne, let her be. If Alysha wants to confide to us anything about Jeff, she'll do so when she's ready."

I silently blessed Jan for her natural peace-making ability and contemplated how much to say to these women who had helped me so often. Best to keep it simple for now.

"Listen. I thank you both for your concern." I chose my words with care. "Jeff and I are going through a rough patch - what you might call a hiccup - in our relationship. We seem to have gone off in different directions but... things, I'm sure will get better."

I waited for a response, but neither spoke. I reached for my glass of wine and took a sip. In the past, I might have prattled on to fill an empty silence but have since learned to be okay with quietness. I used the time to peek at Dianne, who seemed dying to say something. On the other hand, Jan's face showed her concern for me and made me grateful to have her friendship.

Dianne managed to bite her tongue, but Jan broke the silence when she spoke up. "Alysha, we are both so fond of you, and Jeff. It distresses us to see any discord between you two. You know you can come to us - anytime - to talk. Or vent. You have quite a load running this place, plus your career in town. Estelle used to warn me about burning the candle at both ends."

Mention of my grandmother made me smile. I didn't give Dianne a chance to voice her opinion. "Thanks, ladies. Let's change the subject, okay?" I emptied my wine glass and focused on a new topic. The death in town. "Lots of talk all over the place about the death yesterday. Along the lines of what Cassie already gave us. A big setback for the theatre group. And they have no access to the building while the investigation continues."

I kept talking to hold Dianne at bay. "Jan, by chance have you heard anything from the police about who's in charge?"

A few months ago, Jan's nephew, Dakotah - Dax - Young, had been the senior police officer in town. We'd had an interesting relationship, to say the least. He'd since moved on to a new position in Toronto, and I didn't know if Jan kept in touch with his former police partner.

Jan gazed over at me meaningfully while she poured herself a tea. "Yes. I heard from Dax recently. Imagine. As his auntie, I had the pleasure of changing his diapers and now he's a big shot with Toronto Police Service as an Inspector."

"You and your sister must be bursting with pride for him. I'm sure the promotion is well deserved." I only hoped Jan wouldn't make any reference to the awkwardness that existed between Dax and me when he left. And by awkward, I mean Dax's interest in me. A bit more than flirting - unsettling I'd say.

Jan couldn't keep the smile full of pride from her face. "Lots of crime in the big city keeps him busy. Steven Dubois, you remember him, don't you? He has a new partner, and they'll be in charge of enquiries into this new death - under the direction of a senior officer. I'm sure he'll show up here sometime."

Dianne grimaced. "Remember him? Who could forget!"

I knew there were bound to be major disappointments around here because most of the residents, and Cassie, had volunteered to assist with the new theatre venue in various ways. Even Jeff had offered a hand with set construction - he'd delivered paints, plywood, and other lumber to have on site as the renovation project neared completion. Another jab at me. Once again, he managed to find time for just about everything, or everyone, else.

Jan, who is not a busybody but does keep abreast of what is happening in town, added some background, more for my benefit. The Countryside Players were well known in the area and had been successful for decades. "So successful they outgrew their old building and needed a bigger venue. The vacant movie theatre fit their bill, so to speak. Although I've heard some of those who live in the area aren't overly keen on the added traffic it will bring."

She glanced over at Dianne, who had grown quiet since I put the brakes on any more relationship comments. "Ms. Mitchell. Did the bump to your face freeze your tongue now? You might want a bit more cover-up. Purple and yellow don't blend well on your face."

Dianne blinked a couple of times. Her mind must have been wandering. "Right. Yes, a little more make-up would help. Sorry. I was back remembering what caused the bruise in the first place. I'd do it again if I ever hear another derogatory comment about the Patels. Or anyone else who lives here for that matter."

Jan and I exchanged a glance. Where had that come from?

Dianne sipped at her wine. "Makes me think about Minnie, too. I have a lot to make up for when it comes to her. Hearing the Patels being judged made me realize how much judging I did with Minnie as well."

Talk about an old dog learning new tricks! Not that Dianne is old, but it's never too late to make amends. I offered a suggestion. "Here's some food for thought, Dianne. Once she's settled a little more, she might enjoy a day-outing, or a nice long drive with you? After being so reclusive here I bet she'd be surprised to see how Grant's Crossing has grown."

Dianne nodded. "Not a bad idea."

"Oh," I said, "and maybe take Sasitha along as well. She seems to have taken to Minnie. And what's not to like about Sasitha?"

Jan, who naturally mothers one and all under her care, smiled. "Terrific idea, Alysha. Which reminds me. I meant to tell you Frank has offered to get Minnie to all her appointments and will be her advocate with her doctors. He's agreed I can share any pertinent information with both of you."

She started clearing away the glasses and tea things. Our signal the evening news or a favourite TV program was about to start.

Dianne and I promptly jumped up. I laughed and said to Jan, "The saying... Here's your hat, what's your hurry, comes to mind. Okay, we're going. See you tomorrow."

Dianne, though, had the last word. "Tomorrow. I forgot to tell you. Cory Banker is coming for a visit."

CHAPTER SIX

Dianne

Coffee in hand I made my way outside to the veranda for a few moments to enjoy a warmer day than the weatherman predicted. A sweater would be enough to ward off any chill. I love this time of year when the air is so fresh and crisp. But it's the trees, with their stunning colours, that please me. Leven Lodge sits on a rise, with a tree-filled view. This morning the colours were vibrant, and I drank them in. I'd bet we only had a couple of days left to enjoy nature's palette.

Chair cushions hadn't yet been stored for the winter, so I nestled myself into a seat where the sun's rays could reach my face.

Alysha had already left for the day. She hadn't come down for breakfast with the rest of us, so I had no chance to apologize for my unasked-for intrusion into her personal life last night. In hindsight, I should never have bugged her about Jeff. But what's done is done and I'd talk with her later. For now, I had other things on my mind.

Cory Banker. Sixteen, and homeless only a few months ago. We'd met under strange circumstances, to say the least. He'd nearly got me, Alysha, and Nina, killed in a dark alley. We learned about his life as a runaway street kid and the life-threatening experience had been a blessing in disguise for him. And maybe for me, too.

Long story short, he went into foster care with a wonderful family in town. The Cohen's had been happy to allow me a say in Cory's life and I worked with them to help provide clothing (I hoped at almost six foot tall, he'd stopped growing!) and stuff a kid his age liked. Video games for example, and books. The kid loved to read. I was surprised to learn he listed some of his favourite authors as H.G. Wells and George Orwell. But the gifts were conditional. I'd learned he also loved animals and dreamed of becoming a vet one day. So, in exchange for my help,

Cory was coming to Leven Lodge to see if he'd be a good fit working with the alpacas. And if his helping meant it freed up some of Jeff's time, then bonus. Two birds with one stone, you know?

"Morning, sweet cheeks. Mind if I join you?"

"Nina. You going to be warm enough?" Nina loved, to a fault, the colour yellow, and the more fluorescent the better. The summer-weight sweater she wore wouldn't be warm enough for the day. One of her signature scarves, wound around her neck and shoulder like a sling, rippled furiously until a small, quivering, black nose appeared. "Hemingway might be chilly, too."

Nina snuggled her tiny dog closer. "We've only stuck our noses out for a breath of air." She inhaled a lungful of the crisp fall air. "I've got a full day of writing ahead of me. Lily and Rose have been more than helpful. The irony of twins being so different. But the upbringing they had! Well, you'll have to read all about it when the book is published."

"Can't wait, I'm sure."

When Nina had first arrived in the summer, for a temporary six-week writing retreat, she'd wanted to publish a murder story based on what had happened here last year. We soon put a stop to that. Then her short-term stay was extended when Rose and Lily agreed she could write about them. Her time would be up by year's end though, so she'd better get her first draft done pronto. Unless she and Bennett tied the knot - which wouldn't surprise me.

"Tell me what's new with you and Bennett. You two sure spend a lot of time together."

"We do, don't we, chickie. Well, as it happens, Bennett is taking me out for dinner this evening. Such an interesting man. Deliciously appealing if you get my drift. I like my men larger than life. And successful. He's like a great big old cuddly bear." What a salacious smile she wore!

And there it was. After a couple months of hot and heavy, the pace hadn't let up for them. I got it and didn't care to hear more. Fortunately,

I was saved by the bell, or should I say, whimper. Hemingway was trembling. Not cut out for cooler temperatures, or miffed at not being fawned over. He wasn't her number one anymore, or did dogs care about that kind of thing?

"Are you cold, snuggums? I am, too. Let's go back inside and you can get all cozy while I work. Catch you later, sunshine."

Peace and quiet returned and I thought ahead to Cory's visit. I was both nervous and excited at the same time. I'd never been a parent and if you'd told me a year ago, I'd be mentoring a teenager I'd have laughed. But, something about Cory brought out some kind of maternal instincts, and I wanted to do all I could to help him better himself. He'd left an abusive home at fourteen, preferring to rough it on the streets. And he'd dodged the authorities until becoming involved with a couple of murderous thugs back in the summer.

I checked my watch. Nearly eleven. He had no afternoon classes and promised he'd be here just after noon. Which meant he'd need some lunch.

We don't do formal lunches here, but the kitchen is always open to any of us if we want to fend for ourselves during the day. I decided to go see what I could whip up for a growing boy's appetite. Maybe Jan would be around, and I could ask her advice.

***

"No worries, Ms. Mitchell. It's a perfect day for a walk, and don't forget, I'm used to being outside. I enjoyed walking here. But maybe I'll see if I can buy a bike. It'd come in handy."

Cory sat at the kitchen table with Jan and me. She'd put together a hearty sandwich and small salad for him. He'd put on a few pounds and looked healthier than the first time I'd seen him. I knew he'd worked hard to catch up in school as well and his grades showed he had potential to succeed with high marks. He'd come so close to having his life go the wrong way. Okay, I'll admit it. I was proud of myself for whatever part I'd played in his turnaround. But the credit for his life's change of direction was all on him. Life experiences had given him wisdom beyond his sixteen years.

"Classes going well?" I asked.

He finished the last of his salad and nodded. "Um, yeah. I got a 92 in my last science test." He tried to sound like it was no big deal, but the way he smiled told me he was pleased.

"Well done, Cory!" Jan stood up and began clearing away the dishes. He hadn't left a crumb. "Bet you'd like a slice of cake to finish?"

"Yes, please. And thanks for the sandwich."

He looked at me. "Mrs. Cohen said to thank you for the gift certificate to *Books and More*. I'll let you know what I end up buying. Probably won't be anything by Nina Mikado, though."

I chuckled. "I can believe that. Maybe you might want to see if they have anything on alpacas? Jeff and Frank are glad you'll be helping them. I'll take you out back in a minute and introduce you. You can work out a schedule, providing it doesn't interfere with school."

"I'm grateful you'll let me work here. I love animals and this will be the experience I need for university. If I can get my other grades up."

"Cory, you can accomplish anything if you put your mind to it and want it bad enough. And I'm only too willing to help you. Believe me; your help will be appreciated. It gets pretty busy around here at times." I watched him eagerly attack the chocolate cake Jan placed in front of him.

"You know, I don't mind helping out here in the house, too. I can run a vacuum or do laundry. You guys have helped me more than you know. I'd like to return the favour."

Jan came over and put her hand on his shoulder. "I know you had a rough life, young man, but somewhere along the way, you picked up a fine character. I'll talk with Alysha and see if there's something we can work out. And now, shoo! Out of my kitchen. I have work to do, and the alpacas are waiting."

Cory and I strolled to the barn to meet up with Jeff, Philip, and Frank. Cory mentioned he hoped to land a part-time job as a ticket-seller with the new theatre. "If it ever opens. I met that lady who was killed. She was going to get me an interview, but now I don't know what will happen."

"I'll see what I can find out, okay? In the meantime, while I'm impressed you're searching for a job, make sure you don't spread yourself too thin. School work still comes first. Got it?"

"Yes, ma'am. Got it."

"So, what's your take on her? The dead woman. I've heard rumours she might have a lot of people who wouldn't be sad she died."

"She acted okay with me, I guess. Seemed to be busy and then some guy—maybe who does the construction work on the place—interrupted us when we were talking. She went ballistic. I was kind of embarrassed for him, you know?"

I mulled that one over and added it to the comments Cassie had made. Maybe the police had a murder on their hands after all. She didn't sound much like a people person. I put the thought aside as we reached the barn.

"No Frank?" I asked as we saw Jeff and Philip organizing garden implements and empty flowerpots.

"He's gone into town. Should be back any minute. This is Cory, right? Hi, I'm Jeff."

They shook hands. I'd explained to Cory about Philip's autism and Cory, bless him, took it in stride when Philip didn't acknowledge him other than to say, "Frank needs more butter and graphite."

Jeff leaned in. "He means lubricant, not butter. We need it to prepare the tools for the winter. To keep the rust away, you know?"

I handed Cory over to Jeff, who seemed a little quieter than usual. But he was pleasant and welcoming to Cory and I left them to it.

Returning to the house, I came in through the back door which led to the kitchen. Cassie and Jan were discussing supper plans. "By the way, Nina won't be joining us for dinner. In case she hasn't mentioned it."

The front doorbell chimed, and I offered to answer it.

Opening the door, I found DC Steven Dubois and a new face, both in uniform. Dubois was easy on the eyes, but this was no social call. And experience with police here in Grant's Crossing had not always been positive for me. Lightning couldn't strike twice, could it?

"Ms. Mitchell. We're here as part of a murder investigation. May we come in?"

CHAPTER SEVEN

Alysha

After showing two houses to prospective clients, I headed back to the office. Bennett liked to be apprised of everything his realtors were doing so I needed to bring him up to date. Even though he's head honcho of his real estate kingdom and forever on the go, Bennett has a knack for taking the time to make me believe I'm on the right track. His help is crucial for me to achieve my dream of running a brokerage of my own.

I knocked on his closed office door but no reply.

Christine, the office's new receptionist, looked up. "I'm sorry Alysha, Bennett hasn't come back from lunch yet. He mentioned something about a dinner date and might not be back this afternoon. With some woman author, I heard, staying where you live?"

"You mean Nina Mikado?"

A grin threatened to split her face. "Yes, Nina. I think he has the hots for her." She giggled in an annoying schoolgirl manner.

"Not any of our business, Christine. Bennett wouldn't be pleased to hear you talk like this about him." She had a lot to learn about office etiquette, but I wasn't much in the mood to start lessons.

Her face fell and her lower lip quivered. I moderated my tone. "I have some paperwork to finish. When I'm done, they'll need to be filed. You've been shown where they go?"

She nodded and her face brightened. "Yes, of course."

And then she just stood there as if unsure what to do next. I had the answer. "Christine, the phone is ringing. You should probably get it."

She went back to her desk, and I went to mine. I made short order of paperwork, and some outgoing calls, but had still not heard back from Bennett. So, I took my stack of papers out to Christine, where she sat, scribbling phone messages. Bennett's other agent, Ernie Peak, had arrived back at the office. He was on the phone, and I was glad she wouldn't be on her own yet.

"Christine, I'm going home for the day. I'll bring Bennett up to date tomorrow if I don't speak to him later."

She started chattering. "Right, I'll let him know. Oh, the mayor called and wanted to talk to Bennett - should I call him, or leave a message?"

"The mayor? Was it urgent?" I tried not to sound impatient. "What would you normally do if he called?"

"Well, not actually the mayor, like, but his assistant and she says the Town Hall is in an uproar over this recent death at the old cinema. The council had approved the funding for the renovations so, like, I think they're calling it a murder now."

And I thought Cassie took the cake on rambling! She didn't answer my question about why the mayor's office would be calling Bennett, and not for the first time today did I wish Bennett's assistant were here. But she was off on maternity leave and Christine did her best to cover for her while still learning her role. She was a new intern from the local college. Friendly, but gossipy like our Cassie. In front of me her face showed uncertainty and not a hint of a smile.

I began to feel a bit like Jan. "If you're asking for my advice I'd get Bennett on his phone, or at least leave a voicemail. I'm surprised the mayor's office couldn't reach him directly."

"I'll keep calling but..."

"I'm sure he'd want to know the mayor's office needed to speak with him. It must be important."

"Yes, you're right." Her smile reappeared. "Thanks for the advice, Alysha. See you tomorrow."

***

I drove home with the windows down. Perfect weather this time of year was meant to be enjoyed whenever possible. The breeze, carrying faint traces of burning leaves, helped clear my head of office concerns.

In no time I arrived home at Leven Lodge. As I wound my car up the gravel drive, I drank in the comforting picture the house provided, where the trees surrounding the property wore vibrant fall colours, and in the distance, I glimpsed our alpacas in the meadow.

Home. But what the hell! Why was there a police car at our front door once again? I parked and hurried to the veranda where I found Dianne in a state. DC Steven Dubois and another cop were asking permission to come inside.

Relief flooded Dianne's face when I spoke, as I tried to keep the greeting positive. "Good afternoon, Detective, I thought we'd seen the last of the police around here. You'll be giving this place a bad reputation."

Dubois offered a small smile. "Not our intent, Ms Grant. But may we...?"

I ushered the two men and Dianne into an unoccupied front room, away from the crowded front doorway. We passed Rose and Lily, who didn't say a word. Maybe they'd become used to police presence around here. I shut the French doors for privacy, no matter what the police were here for.

Dubois and I began to speak at once, but I let him go ahead.

He nodded and took an at-ease stance. "Alysha, er Ms. Grant. First, I'd like to introduce my new partner, Constable David Truman. Grant's Crossing is his first post." Turning to acknowledge Dianne, he continued. "And this is one of Leven Lodge's residents, Ms. Dianne Mitchell."

Truman tipped his head at me. Whenever the police took a formal name approach, I knew now it meant official business. This younger version of Dubois gave me the impression he'd graduated from the police academy only last month. Tall and slim, his buzz-cut hair was probably brown, but I had to wonder if he's started shaving yet? I resisted the impulse to size him up as an age and personality match to Christine back at the office.

"Constable Truman and I are part of the team investigating the murder in town. We're here to interview all who've been in contact with April Lancashire in the recent past. We understand some of your residents have an interest in theatre participation and may have talked with her in the past few days."

"Wait. You're saying now it is a murder?" I didn't care for the way my stomach had reacted to the news. And by the lack of colour on her face, neither did Dianne. "You've confirmed my suspicion that this is no social call." I straightened my shoulders. "You'll find no murderers here!"

Dubois held up a hand. "No one said anything about a murderer. We're information gathering, that's all." He faced his new partner, who had his pristine notebook at the ready. "Now you can start taking notes, Dave."

His calm manner with his inexperienced partner lowered my anxiety level. "Sorry. Bit of an overreaction. Questions, of course. Who do you need to speak with?"

I glanced over at Dianne. She fidgeted with buttons on her sweater, bursting at the seams to say something. I put a hand on her wrist. "Hang tight, Dianne."

Dubois gave point to Truman, and he raised his pen over his notebook. He coughed and looked at me. "Ms. Grant, we'd like to have a word with Jeff Iverson first, if he's available."

He glanced at both Dianne and me and puffed out his chest. Please don't tell me he's out to prove something to us. I'd cut him some slack, though. We've all been newbies at some point.

He mistook my hesitation for anxiety. "To make it clear, these are preliminary inquiries. No one is being accused of anything. We have to cover all the bases."

In my head, I could hear Dianne say, Thanks, Captain Obvious and didn't dare look at her. I countered with my professional tone.

"Of course, Constable Truman, we'll cooperate fully. You'll find Mr. Iverson in the barn or out in the meadow with the alpacas. Would you like me to show you the way?"

Dubois responded. "Not, necessary, but thank you. We'll find our way."

Referring to his notebook Truman asked me to have Rose Edwards and Cassie DeSouza ready to interview. "We'll talk to them once we return from the barn."

I turned to Dianne. "I know Rose is around, but do you know if Cassie is here?"

She shook her head and answered directly to the constable. "She left about an hour ago to help out in the Crossings Tavern. You know, the one her dad owns?"

Truman scribbled away. "We will contact her later. Thank you."

They left and Dianne and I stood staring at one another in expectant silence until I spoke. "Dianne, what on earth is wrong? You look ready to explode."

"You've no idea, Alysha. No idea at all!" She was breathless and flushed in the face.

"No idea of what? Breathe, and tell me what's going on."

"You don't know what it's like to be suspected of murder. Every time I see the police, I fear they're coming for me. Even though I was cleared of any suspicion it sure spikes my blood pressure. It makes me want to run."

The flush on her face left no doubt she was anxious. "Calm down, Dianne. They're not here to see you, unless you know - knew - April Lancashire?"

"Who? No. No, I don't know her. Sorry, I can't seem to shake this anxiety."

I was spared responding when I heard a gentle tap on the door. "Come in Jan. Maybe you can make Dianne see reason. She's upset because Dubois and his partner are here to interview anyone who's been in contact with April Lancashire - who is now a murder victim. It's likely having the police here so soon after Sloane Jackson's murder has her spooked."

Jan, in her no-nonsense way, hugged her friend, then dispensed her usual sound advice. "Dianne, you never met her, did you? I know you were interested in volunteering to do makeup or something like that. Correct?"

The flush had disappeared from Dianne's face, and she regained control. "Sorry, ladies. You're right, I tend to get anxious when the police are too close for comfort. I'll get over it. No, I've never met the unfortunate woman although I did have an appointment to see her later in the month. To discuss helping out with stage makeup, as you mentioned, Jan."

I brought Jan up to speed. "So, DC Dubois and his new partner, David Truman, want to see Rose and Cassie. They've gone to speak with Jeff now. They know Cassie's at the pub." Questions popped in my head. "Do you know if Nina ever got in touch with her regarding scriptwriting? They never mentioned Nina as someone to interview. Or the Patels - and I know they certainly want to be involved with any theatre productions down the road."

Jan's sigh was born of exasperation. "Cassie will have a field day with these cops. She tattletales so much. As far as I know, neither Nina nor the Patels have met with anyone from the theatre group yet."

I nodded and mentally crossed them off the list. "Jan, would you mind finding Rose? She can wait for them here. Hopefully, the police will be finished with both Jeff and Rose before dinner."

"I can guess where she is. No doubt Lily will want to tag along, but I'll try and prevent it." Jan left and I suggested to Dianne she should leave because Dubois and Truman weren't interested in her and they only made her nervous.

Dianne smiled. Her self-confident, and teasing, persona returned. "On condition you share all the details later. Deal?"

I shook my head. "Dianne, you are incorrigible. Now get out of here before the cops come back. I'll wait here and stay with Rose if she wants me to."

"I need to run to the drugstore anyway, so I'm out of here. It's where I was heading when they arrived. I'll be back before dinner."

Dianne left and I stared out the window waiting for Rose and the officers. Which gave me time to wonder why Jeff had been first on their list?

And once again, best-laid plans, and all that. I'd come home early to try and get Jeff to spend some time with me. Self-pity had taken hold, and I already assumed any time together right now would be all about him and whatever it was the cops wanted to ask him about. I couldn't help but dwell on activity happening at the barn. I'd have to squelch my curiosity until they returned.

My thoughts went on the back burner with the arrival of Rose and Jan, Lily in tow, of course. No surprise there. Jan finally succeeded in persuading her to go back to her room. Lily wore her familiar dejected air, adding more insult to injury as she constantly complained of being left out of everything.

On the other hand, Rose, with her signature fire-engine red lipstick, looked all too eager, in my opinion. She didn't mind being the centre of attention and I deflected most of her questions about why the police were here. Let them handle her.

"But you'll stay with me, won't you?" Then she couldn't decide whether to stand or be seated. I'm sure my eyes rolled more than once. I stayed standing, so eventually, she decided the same. "Am I presentable, Alysha? I didn't have time to change. Always helps to make a positive impression. New lawman in town I hear."

"Um, he's a little young for you, Rose." I laughed and kept to small talk while we waited. Which wasn't long.

Dubois and Truman came forward. I half expected to see Jeff, but no. I assumed he'd stayed out in the back until dinner.

"This is Mrs. Rose Edwards, officers. She has asked me to stay with her."

Once more Truman was given the role of investigator. Dubois readied himself to add more notes, after glancing around the room. Duplicating Truman's note taking?

"Mrs. Edwards, thanks for your cooperation. We understand you met with April Lancashire last Friday. Is that correct?"

Rose's eyes twinkled, reminding me of the wolf who gobbled up Little Red Riding Hood. "Yes, Officer Truman, you are correct." She moved in a little closer. "What do you need to know?"

Truman tugged at his shirt collar. "We, ah, we need to know the reason you met with her. And how you found her mood. Frame of mind."

"Right you are, officer. Let's see. I've offered to help with costume design for the Countryside Players you see, and poor Ms. Lancashire had the task of vetting volunteers I believe. It was our first meeting. I'd never met her before, so I don't know what to tell you about her frame of mind. I thought she came across pleasant enough but focused, to a fault, as if on a tight schedule. Is that the kind of information you want?"

Both men must have been satisfied because they had no more questions and Rose was dismissed. Much to her disappointment, I assumed.

Wisely, they waited till she moved out of earshot before speaking again.

"We'll make our way to the tavern now," said Dubois. He seemed anxious to get on with things. And I was anxious to know what they'd asked of Jeff.

"Before you go - was Jeff helpful to you?"

I didn't care for the look they exchanged before Dubois spoke.

"We're not at liberty to provide details but we may come back to see him later. And, we have asked him not to share what we talked about either. Thanks again."

Ouch. Now the shoe was on the other foot. Last year, the roles had been reversed. The police had spoken to me in confidence, and I couldn't share with Jeff. But surely, I'd get something from him, wouldn't I?

I ushered them out the front door. Dubois gave me a tight smile while his protege preened at being the top cop - for the moment.

The comment about needing to see Jeff again bothered me. So, I made my way to the barn where I found Jeff, with Philip and Cory. They hovered over one of the crias. We'd had two births only a few weeks ago, adding to our herd. Something Jeff was keen to oversee -expanding the herd to eventually make a profit from their fleece.

Jeff rolled his shoulders and swallowed hard. "Alysha. It's Ryker. He's sick and I'm worried about him. I'm going to drive over to Rick's place to see if he has time to come and see what's wrong."

Jeff was still learning about alpacas and his concern for the little one touched me. I tried to reassure him. "I'm sure he can help. He's had lots of experience. But why don't you call him instead. Wouldn't that be quicker? And then we could have a chat about what the cops were after?"

He was wound up tighter than a corkscrew and spoke with impatience which I didn't deserve. "Not now, Alysha. Please. I need to get out of here for a while. The police? I'll tell you about them later. Right now, I'm going to Rick's place."

What the heck had the cops said to him? Something had him on edge - over more than the alpacas I thought.

He spun around and ran for his truck in the driveway. Not even a goodbye kiss! Talk about a cold shoulder - so much for a quiet chat. The alpacas always come first with Jeff!

CHAPTER EIGHT

Dianne

Boy, I had acted damn stupid back there with Alysha. My excuse of needing the drugstore was just that. An excuse to leave. Before the boys in blue came back from the barn. I realized I needed to work on the negative reaction I experienced these days around them. Another memento courtesy of Sloane Jackson I could do without.

I drove up River Road, enjoying the sense of freedom that being behind the wheel provided. I hoped things would work out for Cory. He'd had a rough start in life, but he had goals. And in a way it surprised me I felt invested in him enough to see him achieve his dream. He was a good kid and the brief, but frightening, scare we'd been part of seemed to have put him back on track.

Thinking about him provided a sense of satisfaction. Perfect. He loved books, so my destination changed from the drugstore to *Books and More.* Maybe something on animal care. Could be useful if he stays to work with the alpacas.

I turned the car around and headed back to town. Police tape remained in place. With the old cinema cordoned off, small knots of curiosity seekers remained, and meant gums would still be flapping over the death. Driving by the market brought a flush of embarrassment. It would be a while before I darkened their doors.

I parked and made my way to the bookstore. A bell tinkled over the door announcing my arrival. The first time I'd visited, I'd been astounded at the sheer volume of books the store held! It hadn't changed.

Nina Mikado had made her mark. The cozy and welcoming reading corner featured her books, or at least three of them. How long before she added her expose on the twins, I wondered.

I brushed the thought away and began my search. Deceptively bigger than it appeared from the street, the store held groaning bookshelves which stretched far into the back. The old wooden floor creaked a little as I made my way up and down aisles. Other voices were muted. Books make superb sound insulators. I selected a couple of mysteries I thought might make a welcome addition to the small book collection back at the lodge. Bea McTaggart had loved to read, and she had started adding books, with her reviews, to the large bookcase in the front room. I missed her. A gentle soul, with class.

The shop's bell over the door continued its job of announcing customers coming and going. I finally found some paperbacks on farm animals and even scored a book specific to alpacas. Pleased with a successful hunt, I began to make my way to the cash register when a familiar voice caught my attention.

"Griff. Don't take it so personally. The police are talking to anyone who spoke with April before she died."

Cassie. In a bookstore? Maybe for a cookbook. But who was she talking to? I crept a little closer and found I could just peek through one row of books to see her. And her companion.

Handsome guy, from what I could see. Could be in his thirties. Taller than Cassie, and slim. Locks of chestnut-coloured hair teased his shirt collar beneath a dark grey Gatsby cap. When he turned briefly in my direction, I could see he sported suspenders. And were those kid gloves he wore? A new boyfriend? He seemed a little pretentious. I'd lost track, but this guy didn't fit her usual type.

He was jittery. "I know, I know. You're right. But when they asked me how many times I'd been rejected by her, Dubois gave me a weird look."

"They're police. They suspect everyone. Listen. I'll stick up for you, don't worry."

"You will?" He reached out as if to give her a hug but stopped. "Thank you. She was awful to everyone, Cassie. And I have had leading roles before. I've told you. She could have given me a chance. But oh no. I barely talked with her, and she dismissed me. She likely crossed the wrong person, that's what I'm thinking."

"Shh! You need to keep your voice down. That's why I brought you here from the tavern. Too many ears there."

"Right. Sorry. Anyway, I need to find some cash for a few days. Rent will be due soon and I had counted on getting hired at the market. I even asked your dad if he needed any kitchen help, but no joy this time. I shouldn't have left, then I'd still be a server." He took his cap off and twirled it in his hands. "Say. Any chance the place where you live needs some help?"

I held my breath waiting to see how Cassie would respond.

"I doubt it, Griff. But I'll ask around. I heard the gas station on the road out of town might need someone?"

"Okay. I'll check it out, thanks." His voice brightened. I suspected he had a sunny personality; the type to take life in stride. "And whoever they get to run the auditions, well. I'll try out again. And this time I'll get the part!"

He leaned in to plant a kiss on her cheek, and she pulled back. So, maybe not a boyfriend. "Listen, Griff. I have to get back home to help out with supper. But we'll talk later, okay?"

"Sure, Cassie. I'll be around. Um, maybe we could grab a coffee over the weekend?"

She pushed back her long hair behind her ears. "Not sure. I'm working this weekend. I gotta go, Jan will be waiting."

I watched them leave and thought about how I could best ask Cassie about Griff without admitting I'd eavesdropped on them.

A tap on my shoulder startled me. "Excuse me, I'd like to see these books you've been in front of... for a while."

Oh perfect. Guess who? Janice push-me-in-the-face O'Hare, that's who. Was everyone out to get under my skin today?

The sharp beak on her pinched face sniffed in my direction. "Or are you buying one of these books... to read?"

"I wanted a book on spells, but I dare say you've bought them all." And then I pivoted, hard, and headed for the counter to pay for my purchases. Be quick, be quick.

No one was ahead of me, and I whipped out my debit card. Purchase completed; books bagged. No small talk to the clerk. I couldn't due to holding my breath.

Outside the shop, I exhaled. My hand shook as I dug for my car keys, but I also felt exhilarated at my comeback to the old busy body. Then I deflated. I couldn't brag about my little victory to anyone without it sounding immature. Some days being an adult was no fun at all.

Rats. I slapped my hand against the steering wheel in frustration – and broke a nail. I had time for a quick visit to the nail salon. I bet I'd hear more chatter in there about the murder. Multi-tasker, that's me.

CHAPTER NINE

Alysha

Dinner was almost over and still no sign of Jeff. He'd sent a text saying he needed to stay with Ryker. The text made more sense than Philip's garbled message about a crowd in the barn. "Jeff said no take-out for Ryker or any visitors and sent me here to have supper."

I wasn't sure what Philip's mumble had meant about too many people. Jeff had become better at interpreting Philip and his sayings than me. But because Philip doesn't like being around a lot of unfamiliar people, I gathered someone else was in the barn. Someone unfamiliar to him.

On the other hand, Jeff's text hadn't said he had company. Men. It's either too much information, or nothing.

Laughter erupted at the table, and I brought myself back to pay attention. Something Dianne must have said.

"Oh my, Dianne. You are having such a fun way of telling a story," said Sasitha. The genuine warmth of her smile underscored her gentle personality. "Is this Janice lady truly a witch who casts the spells?"

Bachan smiled. "My beautiful wife doesn't always catch sarcasm so well. But you, Dianne, are masterful in your delivery."

Sarcasm and gossip. Dianne had them in spades. I listened as she entertained the table with her time spent at the nail salon. Tonight, I had no patience to hear her tale. She repeated, and elaborated, the account of how her eye got bumped and bruised. I was tempted to say something but relented when I saw smiles on the faces around the table. What the heck. I might be irritated by her performance, but even Minnie seemed to be enjoying it, so I let it be. Thankfully, Nina hadn't joined us for dinner. I assumed she and Bennett were together. Her input on this would have put me over the top!

Before Jan brought out the dessert, I thought I'd take the opportunity to excuse myself and head to the barn. The longer I hadn't heard from Jeff, the more irked I grew. I've been told I wear my heart on my sleeve, so I didn't need anyone commenting on the irritation I found hard to hide.

"So, you can see why I couldn't resist the comment to Janice." Dianne pushed her empty plate away. "And besides, Halloween isn't far away. We'll make sure we have some treats for her when she knocks."

"Trick or treating is a tradition that can be traced back to the Middle Ages and the rituals of Samhain."

Dianne didn't miss a beat at Philip's scholarly interruption. His skill to match hers!

"Thanks, Philip – heavy emphasis on *my* middle, I suppose?" More laughter and Dianne grinned, soaking up all the attention. Maybe she felt vindicated now. I began to tune her out, until my ears picked up on the mention of Cassie with a new guy. Sounded as if the bookstore had been a treasure trove of fun for Dianne.

Cassie. She goes through boyfriends like... Oh, shut up Alysha. None of my business unless it affects her duties here. Although, considering what Dianne caught during the conversation between her and this guy, Griff, I was curious to know what she and the police had talked about. A more accomplished talebearer than Dianne, I had no doubt we would all soon hear about it.

I left them to their desserts as Rose began to recite her ordeal with the police. "They wanted to know *everything* I could tell them about that poor woman. I hope the information I gave them will help them find the killer!" Guess she forgot I was on hand when she was being grilled. All of two minutes. Seriously - this place is full of drama queens.

I pushed the back door open and headed in the direction of the barn. I pulled my hoodie a little tighter against the chilly air. Jeff was sure to be there, anxious about Ryker. Poor little thing. It's a good thing we have our friend Rick, the alpaca expert, to lend a hand when needed.

But it wasn't Rick who'd come to assist Jeff. As I drew nearer to the barn, I heard a female voice. Someone new in town?

I entered the well-lit barn. "Hi Jeff. You've missed dinner, so I've come for an update on Ryker."

Bent over Ryker, it took him a moment to turn toward my voice as he straightened up. Was it my imagination, or was he annoyed I'd interrupted him? "Er, Alysha, this is Gillian Walker. She's the assistant vet at Dr. Atkins's clinic in town. Lucky for me she'd been visiting Rick when I arrived; she offered to assist with Ryker."

My internal radar pinged as an attractive brunette, wearing a stethoscope, gave me the once over. "Hi. Nice to meet you," was all I got. She never bothered to stand up. Then I was dismissed as she twisted back to continue her examination of our young alpaca.

Yeah, lucky for you Jeff. Is he even going to introduce *me* to her? I moved closer to them as they huddled in the stall. Ryker, about three months old, lay on his side motionless but awake. Long lashes swept his beautiful chocolate-brown eyes. Animals can look sad. The proof lay on the straw in front of me.

I gave up waiting on Jeff. How could he be so inconsiderate of me? And she bordered on rude, as well. "Dr. Walker, I'm Alysha Grant, the owner of Leven Lodge. I don't want to interrupt your care of Ryker but, like everyone else, I'm anxious for an update."

Gillian Walker rose this time from her stooped position over Ryker and turned to me. All six feet of her. Well, okay, not that tall but she peered down at my five-foot-nothing stature as if I was a roach to squash.

We didn't shake hands and she apologized – showing her latex-gloved hand as the excuse. "Can't be too careful." She reached up to wave off a fly near her face. "And who are these others you mentioned? I wasn't aware we needed to issue status reports?"

Formal or what! My shoulders tensed of their own accord. "Oh, perhaps Jeff didn't tell you? Leven Lodge is more than a farm with a herd of alpacas, but we have eight residents, seniors in name only, who call it home. They would be the *others* who are waiting to hear about Ryker."

She nodded. "I see. Fortunately, it's nothing too serious. He's hungry. After examining Mags, we speculate she might be the problem. Ryker is underweight for his age and may not have been nursing well for a few days. He's too early to be weaned, of course. The plan is to monitor him for the next twenty-four hours and provide supplemental feedings." She turned to Jeff. "Are you up for an all-nighter, Jeff?"

A no brainer for Jeff. Where else would he be? Not with me, obviously. The radar pinged harder.

"Sure, sure I'll be here. Now let's check on Mags again. We have some antibiotics for her which should help. An infection with her makes nursing uncomfortable and we don't want to keep them apart any longer than necessary."

They went off without a backward glance, leaving me with the green-eyed monster jabbing at my heart. Jealous? No, I'm not. I'm not.

I shouted at Jeff's back. "Let me know if I can be of help." My offer fell on deaf ears.

I bent down and patted Ryker's head. "Feel better soon." Then I left the barn and headed for the kitchen and some Jan time.

No surprise, I found her busy in the kitchen, clearing up after dinner. I offered my help if she needed it.

"Oh sure, show up when it's all done." Her warm smile evoked a sense of being loved and cared about. If things had ended differently with my Uncle Dalton, she would have been my aunt. Instead, we're steadfast friends and I can depend on her for sound advice.

"What's up, little one? Something on your mind? Your face has the look of someone who's lost their best friend."

I poured myself a cup of tea from the large teapot Jan always had going. I perched on a stool by the kitchen's island. As I sipped at the tea, I wasn't quite sure how to begin. "I think I might have, Jan, and I don't know what to do about it." My voice had grown tight, and I blinked hard.

Jan stayed quiet and joined me with a cup of tea. When she finally spoke, her voice was soft and full of concern. "Whenever you're ready I'll listen. Cassie's out tonight and everyone else is busy so we won't be interrupted. I can tell something is troubling you."

Perceptive as always. I sighed. "It's Jeff. I suspect we're drifting apart. We're not sharing our lives anymore. I'm sure I'm to blame as much as he is." My heart hurt with each word. "Maybe because we're both wrapped up in our own interests. I'm so busy with my career ambitions and he can't see anything but alpacas."

"Alysha, that's part of any relationship. Give and take."

"But not the amount of neglect I've been feeling lately. Get this! Tonight, he's staying in the barn to watch over Ryker, who is sick, yes. But an assistant vet, who is gorgeous, will probably be keeping him company."

Jan tilted her head. "Ah, so you're jealous he has the company of another woman while tending to a sick animal? Oh, Alysha. That's not like you."

It was my turn to stay quiet while I thought about what she had said. I hesitated before answering her comment. "If you had seen this young, and willowy brunette - Gillian Walker - you'd understand. She towers over me and has all the confidence in the world. So, her word rules. She says they need to stay and give Ryker extra feedings and keep an eye on him!"

My voice had risen, and Jan countered with a question. "What's wrong with the alpaca then?"

I had to recall what I'd been told. "Something about a blocked teat with Mags and she needs antibiotics."

"So not life threatening for either? That's good news. But you haven't said how Jeff reacted to the advice given by this paragon of beauty and intellect. Other than he's agreed to be on duty with her?"

"That's just it, don't you see? Jeff says nothing. We don't talk. I don't think we're on the same page anymore." What I was about to say next formulated itself in my brain with almost no effort, and the realization shocked and saddened me. "I admit to jealousy when I first saw her working alongside the man I considered my soulmate."

"And then?" prompted Jan when I had trouble speaking.

I lifted my eyes from my teacup. "This will sound corny, but the jealous feelings were pushed aside by an overwhelming sense of relief."

"Relief?"

"I guess what I mean is that it's kind of a crossroads, at least for me. And maybe we shouldn't be together anymore so we can both follow our dreams." I took a deep breath. "So, where do I go from here?"

Jan moved over to me and wrapped her arms around me, not saying a word for a few moments. When she finally spoke, it was with hesitation. "Little one, I'm not the best one to advise you on your love life. This is something you both must work out. I will say this. It's all part of life's process. Part of growing as a person and finding out who you are. Take it slow and the answers will come to you."

I stared into Jan's eyes and saw only compassion. What a wonderful friend to have. I returned her hug with a squeeze that I hoped would speak volumes to her.

"I'm drained, now. Thank you so much for listening." I pushed the stool back under the island overhang. "It's time to call it a night. We'll see what tomorrow brings."

As I reached the door to make my way upstairs Jan lightened her tone. "You'd better not share too much with Dianne or she'll set you up with a new suitor."

She'd made me smile.

I entered the apartment Jeff and I shared. Unbidden, the image of me being here on my own flashed in my mind. I could do this, but Jeff and I needed to talk. I wasn't sure how he'd react to my revelation of our relationship. I toyed with the idea of dealing with paperwork but couldn't concentrate. I made myself some warm milk, with a touch of vanilla, and took it to drink in bed.

No matter what, like the Grant family motto - I would *Stand Fast*.

CHAPTER TEN

Dianne

"Hi Cassie. Got a minute?"

Our scatter-brained cook, keys in hand, was about to head into town for supplies. She'd managed to avoid talking with anyone about her police experience yesterday. Probably Jan's doing. Cassie tends to share news which might be better kept under wraps. But seeing as I had already overheard part of her experience, I'd use it as the opening.

I was in the driveway, cleaning my car. One last healthy attack with the vacuum cleaner, and garden hose, before winter. And I needed to see about getting the snow tires on. Mid-October was never too soon for a first snowfall.

Cassie changed direction and came my way. "Great morning for this, Dianne. I can give you my car keys when you're done?"

We laughed. "Nope, one car a season is plenty for me. Maybe that new boyfriend of yours can take care of it for you?" Was that subtle enough?

"Huh? What boyfriend? I'm not seeing anyone right now. You're mistaken."

"Oh, guess I misread what I saw yesterday. You, in the bookstore, with a kind of cute guy?"

"What – Griff? Oh, no way, Dianne. He's no boyfriend of mine." She blushed slightly. "Although, I imagine he might like to be. He's not my type, so it's not happening." Then she blinked. "You saw us? I didn't see you?"

I shook out the car mats, pretending this was only idle conversation. "I didn't want to intrude. You both were in a serious conversation. I figured it had to do with the police and the murder?"

Cassie looked over her shoulder and lowered her voice. "Yes, you're right. Griff has been interviewed by the police. He'd talked with April not long before... before she was found. They seemed interested when Griff admitted he'd been upset with her at not giving him a chance to try out for parts in a new production."

"How interested?"

"You know how they are, right? Especially after your experience with them. They grab hold of any kind of suspicious behaviour and next thing you know. Boom! You're arrested!"

She didn't have to remind me. "Right. Anyway, do you think he had anything to do with it?"

Cassie took a step back. "Dianne, really? Listen, far as I know, Griff wouldn't hurt a fly. In fact, it's one of the things that puts me off him, you know? He's too passive, and generally just a nice, bland, guy. Not much motivation or ambition. Like a drifter. He'd be more likely to cry in a corner, than bash someone's head in."

More detail! "Her head was bashed in?"

"Yeah, I probably shouldn't have said anything. Don't repeat it to anyone, okay? But the police said they found a two-by-four next to the body." She stopped and once again ensured nobody was around to eavesdrop. "Sounds like the murderer tried to hide her under some sheets of plywood. Anyway, they want Griff to come in today and offer to be fingerprinted to rule him out. I bet everything was covered in blood!"

"You don't have to sound so enthusiastic, you know. Did they question you as well?"

She frowned. "Not so much. I've only talked to April once, on the phone, to discuss possible catering opportunities. My dad and I thought we could do up sandwiches, you know, for whenever the theatre is up and running and has cast rehearsals. Including light snacks for the ticket buyers for pre-show, and intermissions. They want to get a liquor license as well. Did you know that?"

Having a liquor license wasn't high on my list of need-to-know items at the moment. As I listened to her, I tried to figure out how I could learn from Alysha about Jeff's police interview. She'd left before breakfast, and Jeff, as usual, kept a low profile out in the back. He did spend an inordinate amount of time with those alpacas. I know one of them was under a vet's care, but still. I couldn't even remember the last time he and Alysha had gone for a run together.

Cassie must have twigged that I'd lost interest in her information leak, and she jangled her keys for effect. "Listen, I gotta get going. Need some fresh fish for dinner. Catch you later." She glanced up at the sky. "And if it rains, I know who to blame – you and your car wash."

"Funny girl," I retorted and made to throw a rag at her. She laughed and went on her way.

There wasn't supposed to be rain, but who knew for sure. The sky had clouded over quite a bit, and the temperature had dropped. More than enough motivation for me to finish up, cutting a few corners as I went.

I just finished putting the hose and bucket away, when Nina, in her fluorescent yellow sports car, drove up and parked beside me.

"Nice job, chickie. I'd offer to have you wash my baby, but I'll leave it to the experts."

I ignored the jab. "Long time no see, stranger. Were you even here last night?"

"Keeping tabs on little old me?"

"Seeing as Minnie no longer does, someone should."

She opened the passenger door of her car and scooped Hemingway up and snapped on his glitter-laden lead. "Time for a tinkle, baby, before we go inside."

She let the dog sniff a few feet from her car and watched his toileting, rather than answer my question, I noticed. "What a good little snuggums. Let's go get you a treat."

"Um, last night, Nina?"

A devilish grin lifted the corners of her mouth, and she laid a maroon-lacquered nail to her lips. "A lady never tells." Then she tucked the dog under her arm and breezed into the house.

Whatever. She'd spent the night with Bennett, big deal.

I finished working on my car and went in search of a coffee. Cory was coming back after school, and I had those books to give him.

***

"Thanks for these books, Dianne. Seeing as I 'll be helping out with the alpacas, these'll come in handy." He tucked the books into his backpack.

I'd met Cory as he arrived for his daily chores, and we walked together toward the barn. He was over the moon at the part-time job offered him by Jan and approved by Alysha. Two days a week after school and every other Saturday. He'd promised Jan she could count on him for help in the house as well. I kicked at some leaves as we strolled. Maybe Frank would show him how to use the leaf blower.

"The alpacas are fascinating. And I like Jeff. He's easy to work with."

"What about Philip? You might have to be patient with him. It takes a while to sometimes figure out what he's saying."

"He's cool. I kind of like being able to talk with a teacher who's not my teacher, you know?"

"I have a hunch they'll be glad to have you on hand as well. What happened with the police and Jeff yesterday? I had to go into town and missed seeing them leave."

At the mention of police, Cory stopped walking. Something we shared in common - our negative reaction to them. I knew we both had to get over it.

"At first, I thought they were coming to get me! And I almost ran, but Jeff calmed me down. And the one cop asked me how I was doing in school and stuff – which made me feel better."

"You're on the right side of them now, Cory. I'm still skittish around them, but it's getting better. One day I'll tell you the reasons." We stopped by a fence to watch the alpacas in the field. "How was Ryker when you left yesterday?"

"I'd say much better. Look." He pointed the young alpaca out to me because I couldn't tell them apart. Ryker nuzzled at his mother, a good sign, I assumed.

"Back to the police for a sec. Were you able to hear what they said to Jeff?"

"Nope, they took him over to a corner away from us. I couldn't hear what they were saying. But I did see one of the cops point to a pile of lumber and then Jeff shook his head - hard. One cop wrote in his notebook and then they left. After they left, Jeff didn't say anything other than talk about the alpacas. I figured it was because I was there and new to everything?" He smacked his palm on the fence. "Oh, but I did hear one thing. As the cops were leaving, Jeff shouted out to them to talk to someone named Wallis."

"Hi Cory! Come on, I've lots to show you today." Frank had spied us at the fence and any more questions I might have had were postponed. The name Wallis sounded familiar, but my mind wouldn't cough up any more information.

"Make sure you get something to eat before you leave. We usually have dinner around six, so come to the house with Jeff at dinner time. I'll let Jan know."

I left them to it and turned back. And then I remembered. Brock and Sheridan Wallis. Husband and wife contractors who owned Brodan Contracting just outside of town. I remembered seeing their name on the construction sign outside the theatre.

Him I didn't know for certain, but I'd made the acquaintance of Sherri Wallis not long after moving here. Our manicure appointments at *Heaven Scent* had jived more than once and we'd struck up a casual friendship of sorts. We were about the same age, but I didn't assume she was drawing pension cheques yet, like me. We met for a coffee now and then. Their business seemed to be going well. Hmmm. Should I give her a call and see if another coffee was needed?

I might have time before dinner. My thoughts were on making an excuse to meet up, when I saw Alysha pull into the driveway. We hadn't talked much lately, and she wasn't her usual upbeat self, at least in my opinion.

Troubles in paradise, I'd say. Another reason I'm glad to have never gone the marriage route again after the big mistake I'd made in my twenties. Much prefer my own company, thank you. But I didn't wish bad times on Alysha and Jeff. I liked them both.

I waved to her from a distance and thought she might wait for me to catch up. Instead, she went straight inside. Would either of them join us for dinner? I'd know in a couple of hours.

CHAPTER ELEVEN

Alysha

I hadn't slept well last night but I couldn't beg off work. Dealing with paperwork and answering emails wasn't working as a distraction. Thank goodness I had no clients today as my mind couldn't settle on purchase agreements and conditional financing arrangements. My love life, as Jan calls it, is in tatters and I'm not sure what to do about it. The man whom I've lived with and loved as a partner in running the Lodge has all but checked out on me. This is not what I'd envisioned for my life.

"Earth to Alysha."

I started when Bennett entered my office and plonked himself down in a chair opposite me. "Sorry, Bennett. Things on my mind. So how are you today?"

"I'm a-okay. In fact, everything is peachy keen." Bennett grinned from ear to ear.

Peachy keen? Is that one of those old folks' expressions? I shot him an inquiring look.

"And I've you to thank."

"What are you talking about?

He leaned forward. "This is overdue, but you're the one who introduced me to the most amazing woman. I can't believe how well we've clicked in such a short time. You know, she's really something. Fireworks and kitten all rolled up in one. I might even steal her away from your lodge." He leaned back in the chair, smiling at some kind of mental image I didn't want to know about. "But one step at a time."

Nina Mikado – otherwise known as Hilary Crocket in her non-writing circles. Larger than life and not afraid to speak her mind. I'd agree with him that she is something, all right. "I'm glad things are working out, but it's still kind of early to be thinking long-term relationship, isn't it?"

"At my age, long-term is all relative. Neither of us are getting any younger."

Wow, wait until this gets out at the dinner table. But they won't hear it from me! I don't know who will have the most fun. Dianne, or Nina if she learns Bennett has been singing her praises.

He stood. "But I mustn't keep you. I must get back to the mayor. He's asked my opinion on the validity of the grant given to the Countryside Players by council. This murder at the cinema has them all on edge. And the police are still hunting for suspects and a motive, I believe."

I was relieved at the change of topic. "Yes, they're still investigating. DC Dubois questioned some of the residents who had met with the poor woman." And also, Jeff! "So, what will you tell the mayor? Surely funds wouldn't be withdrawn. The town council needs to learn more before deciding to cancel the grant - if that's even an option?"

Bennett hesitated and turned back to me, still grinning. "You are decisive Alysha and I trust your judgement. The mayor will hear exactly what you just said. But the police will have to move soon with some results so Grant's Crossing can get back on track with getting the theatre open and selling tickets. It's quite a big investment. And potential tourist draw."

Bennett left and I contemplated what he'd just said. Imagine, my opinion matters to someone. And decisive! I should be able to use some decisiveness in my personal life.

I tidied my desk and left the office for home. With any luck, I'd have the talk with Jeff we've both been putting off.

***

I saw Dianne as I arrived but decided to go straight to our apartment. Her bad-mouthing can be as bad as Cassie's and I wanted to avoid it.

I couldn't wait to get into some casual gear. Not so long ago, it had been routine for Jeff and me to either kick back and enjoy a beer, or go for a run, at day's end. Not so much lately.

Surprise, surprise. Jeff lay sprawled on the sofa, his sockless feet dangling over one end. He might be dozing, but I wasn't in a charitable frame of mind to let him be.

I closed the door with a little more force than usual. "Oh, you're home. I wasn't expecting you here. You're usually stuck in the barn at this time of day." I tossed my work stuff on a chair and tried to clamp down on the fault-finding tone I wanted to use. "And how was your all-nighter? Is Ryker better after your ministrations and the vet's care?"

Jeff blinked and sat upright, rubbing his eyes. "And who pissed in your cornflakes this morning?"

His accusatory tone, not unlike my own, was embarrassing to hear. He softened the edge with his next words, and I'd have to do the same. "Gillian was there to help with Ryker, and I had a responsibility to stay there as well."

I made myself sit next to him on the sofa and tried to keep my voice calm. "I'm not interested in Gillian. It's *your* behaviour lately I don't understand." I paused, knowing I had arrived on the verge of no-turning-back. "Things have changed between us, and we need a serious discussion of our future together."

He studied his feet for a moment, and then looked up. Those magnetic eyes I'd first fallen in love with, were so sad. "That's the reason I'm here now. I know we need to talk." As if he, too, realized the cliff we stood on, he changed topics. "Ryker is nursing again. Mags had an infection and is why she stopped feeding him. Gillian said she'll be fine, but to keep an eye on her."

Again, with the alpacas. I bit my tongue. It wasn't their fault. I decided a few minutes to stall couldn't hurt. "Give me ten minutes to change out of my work clothes and then we'll talk. About everything.

But think on this. We haven't arrived at this point overnight, so I need to understand, Jeff. And I don't want to hear about Gillian either."

Was that decisive enough?

I shut the bedroom door and decided on a quick shower. Then I put on my running gear. I had an idea a run would be needed later.

But run to what? To calm down, let loose frustrations or just run for old times' sake. It had been a while. I texted Jan to say we'd not be there for dinner.

I found Jeff pacing the floor when I came out of the bedroom. Under normal circumstances, he's the most relaxed and placid person I know. Pacing is out of character for him - he had to be upset. Was there something I had missed? My nerves tightened, and I wasn't quite sure how this would play out, so I started with some common ground. "I'll have one of those beers if you've not finished them all."

I sat down in my favourite chair where I had a view to the driveway as it made its way to the main road. Dusk had fallen and the wind had picked up, with clouds hanging heavy. Something like my mood. Jeff handed me a beer and sat opposite me.

I toyed with the label and began to tear at it, gathering my thoughts. "Jeff, let me speak first, please?" He nodded, so I continued. "I'm not sure what has happened between us, but we have lost what we had when we took over the Lodge. I believed, and I think you did too, that we would always be together, but... I'm not blaming you. Something is broken and I'm not sure we can fix it."

The silence was awful. Regret mixed with guilt tugged at my conscience. Oh, what have I done? He's one of the kindest, most loving people I've known, and now... Maybe I wasn't paying attention. "Jeff, please say something."

"Aly, I, I'm not good with words as you know. You deserve better than I've been lately. I'll try and explain, if I can."

My blood ran cold, and I apprehensively told him to tell me what was on his mind. Within seconds, I wished I hadn't.

"You asked me not to talk about Gillian but... she's the reason we're having this talk."

I managed to blurt out. "What do you mean?" Although my hackles had already given me a premonition of what he was going to say, I said no more and kept quiet while he continued.

"We met about three months ago at Rick's place. Our mutual love of the alpacas, and, well, it just happened."

"*What* just happened?"

"About the time you started at Bennett's office. We talked about the alpacas and their welfare and increasing the herd. We enjoy each other's company. We..."

Whatever expression I had on my face made him stop for a moment. But he just had to finish the sentence, didn't he?

"... fell in love."

I couldn't speak - I could barely breathe. After a few seconds he carried on.

"Babe, you know I wouldn't hurt you for the world. I *have* been happy with you here, but I want to work more with animals. Gillian and I have a plan."

I tried to stop the shaking that threatened to overtake me and struggled for control of my voice. "A plan, a *plan*? So that makes the whole thing fine, does it? And you have been seeing her for three months? Well, here is what you can do right now. First, stop calling me babe. I think the name belongs to another now, doesn't it?"

I took a deep breath. The next plunge was unstoppable. "Right, then. Here's the deal. Seeing as we can't live together anymore, I suggest you pack up your belongings and be out of this apartment by the time I get back from a run."

Jeff's mouth opened, and the colour drained from his face. No matter that he was stricken at my words, I determined to be decisive. I steeled myself not to react to the plaintive tone of his voice.

"But where will I go and what about the alpacas? You know how much I love them. I need to take care of them."

"Why don't you call your Gillian and start working on your plan." My voice had gone up an octave and I bordered on tears. No way would I let him see me cry.

I managed to keep a semblance of logic and made an offer. "You can continue to work with the alpacas until we come to some arrangement. Now I'm off for a run so be gone before I return. Anything you can't take, let me know where to send it."

"I'm sorry, Alysha. So sorry." His voice quavered.

"So am I. Goodbye, Jeff."

I shut the door none too gently and was soon pounding the pavement. If it rained, I'd hit the coffee shop, or tavern. Drowning my sorrows held some appeal.

CHAPTER TWELVE

Dianne

Supper last night had been as unbearable as that first meal we'd had together after Dalton died. Sombre, with some tears and sad faces all around. Jeff has left the lodge because he and Alysha have split up. When the news had filtered down to us, Jan admonished one and all to keep out of it and to give both Alysha and Jeff space. She had stood in her kitchen doorway, arms crossed, and spoke to all of us at the dinner table.

"And I don't want to hear anything about taking sides. Both Alysha and Jeff are important to me. Understood?" When Jan's brook-no-argument voice surfaced, no one dared disagree.

She and Jan had spent a couple of hours together last night. I didn't think they'd deliberately shut me out, because I had gone straight to my room after dinner, where I called Sherri Wallis to set up a coffee date. I debated heading downstairs, but decided I'd keep to myself for the rest of the evening. A trip to the kitchen around midnight for a glass of milk found Jan doing the same thing. That's when I learned she and Alysha had talked.

"She will tell you what's happened when she's ready. We thought you'd retired for the evening so didn't bother you."

"It's okay, Jan. I guess neither of us are surprised, but it's upsetting for all of us. Jeff is a likeable guy, and they made a cute couple. I'll see her before long."

We clinked our glasses of milk and said no more.

And this morning? Well, Alysha had left before anyone else was up.

I went back to my room after breakfast. I had a copy of the morning's Gazette to see what was new with the murder investigation and other interesting town news. According to police they were seeking persons of interest and confirmed the death had taken place late afternoon or early evening Sunday. She'd been found the next day.

The gloomy atmosphere and mundane small talk around the breakfast table made me restless, leaving me at loose ends for a couple of hours until I could meet with Sherri.

I settled into my chair by the window. Dark clouds scudded across the sky, pushed by winds that had picked up since daybreak. Leaves swirled about and if rain joined the wind, most of the beautiful leaves would be on the ground. I sighed. The day had a bleak sadness all about it.

***

Two hours later I drove into town and parked near the *Java Hut*. Rain pelted me as I hurried to get inside. Thunder rolled on the heels of a lightning flash. Not a great day to be out, but I was here now.

I looked around, but Sherri hadn't arrived yet, so I ordered my coffee and found a corner table with a view to the street.

Sheets of rain slashed against the window and the blurry shape of a truck parking caught my attention - Sherri. The lightning flashed again, and I glimpsed her, behind the wheel, smashing her hand against it.

Fantastic - someone else having an *exceptional* day, too. Something stronger than coffee would have been a better choice.

A gust of wind blew in as she came inside. She was soaked, her long black hair plastered to her head. I grabbed a handful of serviettes from the table dispenser and waved her over.

"What a downpour!"

"Here, these might help dry you off. I'll get your coffee. Want anything with it?"

She took the tissues and began mopping her face. "If they have any chicken soup, I'll take some, thanks."

Chicken soup sounded satisfying, so I placed an order for two.

More sodden customers entered and soon every table was occupied. I put the tray of soup and coffee down on our table.

"Guess this weather impacts your work?"

"Today it sure does. We have three new builds outside of town. Framing was supposed to happen today, but not in this weather. I would have gone to the theatre reno but it's still off limits. Time is money!"

We'd only met a handful of times and I'd never seen her upset. I'd take the theatre angle. "Any idea when the cops will free it up so you can get on with business?"

She pulled apart a dinner roll. "That will depend on my ever-loving husband. Who right now is AWOL."

"You don't know where he is?"

She put her spoon down, opened her mouth as if to speak, and then must have thought better of it because she went back to her meal. I couldn't resist.

"Does this happen on a regular basis?"

She sighed. "Dianne, to be honest, I don't know you all that well, do I?"

She had me there, but I persisted. "True, but sometimes that's a good thing. I can be objective because I don't know you well and have never met your husband."

"I don't know. This murder has thrown our schedule way off track. We make allowances for cost overruns and delays, but no one would have predicted this kind of delay. I'm just frustrated, that's all."

She spooned more soup into her mouth. She probably needed to vent so I gave her some time and worked at finishing my own bowl of soup – which wasn't nearly as hearty as Jan's!

"We've had the business for more than twenty years. It's been hard work and we sacrificed a lot to keep it going at times. But damn it anyway!"

Her raised voice drew some attention, and she toned it down. "You ever been married, Dianne?"

"Once. Too young, it didn't last more than a year. Haven't had much luck with relationships. But this isn't about me."

She stared at me over the rim of her coffee cup. Still considering what, or how much, to tell me, I'd bet.

"Brock and I have been married almost thirty-five years. Not always been perfect, but we get along, and we have our business, which is successful." She fished in her pocket for some tissue. "And I've always tolerated his betting on the horses and poker games. Because he never lost!"

Oh, oh. Money problems. The death knell for a lot of relationships. "His luck ran out?"

She laughed. "What an understatement. For the last year, he's been running up debts all over the place. And I might still not know about it, except for April."

Hold on now. April – the murder victim? I leaned in closer. "What happened?"

"She called me last week to report some issues with invoices being paid. She is – or was – the treasurer for the Countryside Players. Anyway, she brought it up with Brock. Stupid. She should have talked to me. I run the accounts. But Brock generates the invoices and does have access to business funds."

"What about the invoices?" I had an inkling where this might lead, but let Sherri tell the details.

"I started to review the accounts since we took on the theatre project. April was right. Invoices were being padded and Brock's been skimming the extra to, I assume, pay off his debts. When I confronted him, he blew a gasket." She glanced around and lowered her voice. "He was so angry at April for telling me. That's when he stormed out of the house, the day she was killed. And I haven't seen him since."

"Do the police know this?" What I really meant to say was - had she reported him as missing.

"Not yet."

"Um, do you feel he had anything to do with her murder?"

Her lower lip trembled, and she started to cry. "I'm beginning to think I never knew him like I thought I did. I don't know, I just don't know. I'm scared to think he might have."

"Listen, Sherri. No matter what you presume might have happened, or not, I think you should go talk to the police before they get to you first. Even if it all looks circumstantial about your husband, they'll get to the bottom of it."

She wiped tears away and gave me an unbelieving look. "Right, as if."

"I, uh, I'm talking from experience."

I had her attention, and I gave her the condensed version of being under police suspicion earlier this year with the murder of my one-time lover, Sloane Jackson.

She began to gather her things and managed a weak smile. "I can't see you ever murdering anyone. But Brock, well, let's just say he's had times when stress got the better of him and has made the acquaintance of the police."

I didn't like the sound of that and wasn't sure how to respond.

She stood, and I hurried to get my own stuff ready to leave. "I appreciate the input, Dianne. And I guess you're probably right, but he is my husband, right? And I love him. But I don't know whether to be worried he's missing because something's happened to him, or because he's involved with the murder." She put on a brave face. "Thanks for the soup and coffee."

We headed toward the door and prepared to be drenched once again. I put my hand on her arm. "Sherri, please think about it. The police will ask. Your husband is missing for nearly a week – that's bound to get their attention. And if I can help, let me know?"

She nodded, pushed open the door and ran for her truck. Before I made the run to my car, I realized talking with her had made me forget about Alysha's split from Jeff. I'd swapped one set of relationship troubles for another.

I got into my car, waiting for the engine to warm up so I could turn on the heat. Being wet and cold brought me to shivers. Never mind, I figured topics of conversation back at the lodge would soon warm me up.

CHAPTER THIRTEEN

Alysha

The weather matched my disposition. Grey and dreary. Not the best of days to be showing houses in a favourable light. Rain had been forecast for the next two days, but better than snow I suppose. I needed something to keep my mind off Jeff leaving yesterday. I'd glimpsed him briefly, entering the barn, as I left for work this morning. I loved the alpacas, but I can't talk about them ad nauseum.

Tears weren't far away, prodded by jealousy, as I envisioned Jeff sharing alpaca time with someone probably more interested in them than I. But I was the one who'd set him free, so what did I expect?

Starting my workday earlier than usual this morning gave me the excuse I needed to avoid questions from Dianne and anyone else. I know they'd only mean well, but they would miss him. I wasn't ready to be on the receiving end of sympathy and awkward silences. They'd miss his barbecues, too. Had I done the right thing?

I couldn't avoid talking to Dianne, though. She'd guessed right about problems in paradise. In her own way, she was a comfort to me, as was Jan. I'd need to lean on my friends to get through this.

A knock at my door brought Bennett Howes in front of my desk.

"'morning, Bennett, can I help you?"

My mentor took a seat in front of me. He tugged at his blazer in vain; it would never close over his girth. "I thought I might be of help to you."

"Sorry? How do you mean?" I waved my hand at a pile of papers. "I'm caught up with all the enquiries for new listings. Is there something specific you wanted to talk about? Problems with me?"

He continued to fuss with his clothes, not making eye contact. For someone who'd been given an extra-large dose of confidence from birth, he looked uncomfortable.

"Alysha, this is a small town and people gossip. I'm probably party to more things than I should be. I am sorry to have heard about your breakup with Jeff. If you need to talk or take some time..."

Stunned, I could only stare at him. Was it being spread all over Facebook, too? Not even twenty-fours had passed since Jeff had left!

I couldn't answer him and started opening desk drawers as a diversion. A tear plopped onto my hand, and I reached for a tissue.

"Oh my God. I'm sorry. I'd no idea you'd be this upset, or I'd never have mentioned it. Please forgive a bumbling fool."

A few tissues later and I regained control. "Not your fault. Small town rumour mill at its finest, right? Can I ask how you learned of this newsworthy information about my personal life?"

When he hesitated to reply, I filled in the blanks myself. "So, I'm guessing Nina couldn't help herself. Always searching for a story."

He reached a hand across the desk to pat mine. "Please, don't be mad at her. This isn't a story angle for her. She's concerned for you and thought some time away from work might help." He pulled his hand back and finished by adding she'd offered to be a shoulder for me if I wanted.

I was touched when I saw the concern on Bennett's face. "Please thank Nina - or Hilary as you prefer - but I'll be fine. I'd just like my privacy respected."

"Of course. I understand." He drew an imaginary zipper across his lips, and I smiled.

"Now, is there some business we can discuss? How about your call to the mayor?"

"Of course, the mayor."

Relieved to be back on neutral ground, I let Bennett fill me in.

"Council's still arguing about the money given to support this theatre expansion. Legally, the money is now in their hands. I'm all for it and as a member of the Historical Society, I'd love for it to succeed. Because it's an historic building, I'm happy to see the old cinema given new life, while protecting its heritage. Too many with tight wallets on the board, and town council, for my taste. Looking for a loophole to recoup finances. All over now but the shouting."

"Glad to hear it. Some of the residents are anxious for the new stage to be up and running. They want to volunteer in some way. I try to find new activities to keep them occupied." I had a sudden thought. "Say, do you like to barbecue? Leven Lodge may need someone to take over grill chef duties, which Jeff often did."

Bennett laughed. "You have the wrong boy. Thanks for the offer but I would only provide burnt sacrifices."

I felt hopeful that if I could mention Jeff's name in a light-hearted way, I'd be okay after all.

"The mayor is more concerned the murder be solved, and fast. Last I heard, the police have no suspects."

"Did you know April Lancashire?"

He didn't meet my eyes for a moment. When he spoke, his words were measured. As if he felt guilty speaking ill of the dead.

"Met her a few times over the years. And then of course, recently because of the town's financial support. I love live theatre and often attended productions she'd been involved with. As far as I know, she ran a tight ship with the Countryside Players. They showed profit to be eligible for the grant money match. So, I doubt they'd ever been in debt with her at the helm as treasurer."

We sat in silence for a moment out of respect for her, then I told Bennett about the authorities visit to Leven Lodge.

"The police came to the lodge to interview anyone who'd spent recent time with her. DC Dubois and his partner are quite thorough. They talked with Jeff as well and said they might come back. I'd hope once they finish with the crime scene, they'll release the theatre, and the renovations can continue. As they say - the show must go on. But getting a suspect into custody would do more to calm things down."

"I certainly hope so. Sounds like the police are talking with anyone who knew her. I should be prepared, too. They'll know I had dealings with her over the grant money." He pursed his lips. "And Hilary as well. She'd offered her assistance with script writing, which April welcomed. So, I'd better give her the heads up about the police."

I chuckled "Don't you worry about Nina. She knows how to handle the police, and men in general."

A grin spread across his face—I'd never noticed those deep dimples before—and his eyes twinkled. "I concur with your assessment. She's a pistol, alright. And she'll be absent from your dinner table, again, this evening. We'll be having dinner at my place. Stop right there! I can see you want to comment!"

My grin might have matched his, and I was happy we'd be wrapping up this impromptu meeting on a lighter note than it started. I regretted my earlier tearful outburst.

My phone rang. "Alysha Grant. Can you hold, please?" I turned to Bennett who had risen from his chair. "Back to business." I ventured a further comment. "It's obvious you've fallen for Nina and not just because you've mentioned it once or twice. Does this mean I'll be advertising for a tenant to take her room anytime soon?"

Bennett couldn't keep the grin off his face. "That would be telling, wouldn't it?" Oh, boy. He had it bad. I determined not to dwell on her indiscretion about my life. Who am I to judge?

I waved him out of my office and picked up the phone. "Thank you for holding. How can I help you?"

***

By lunchtime the rain had stopped but clouds left the sky overcast.

My 2:30 appointment had cancelled, leaving the rest of my day clear. No more excuses. Time to see about some quality time with Jan and Dianne - and answer their questions. It was still early enough to give Jan advance notice about dinner. I picked up the phone and called her with my suggestion for a night out.

"Nina won't be there for dinner, so it would only leave the twins, Minnie, and Philip, and the Patels for Cassie to look after. And you know Sasitha would be more than happy to give Cassie help if she needed it." I persisted with Jan – to overcome her reluctance about leaving Cassie in charge on short notice. "Listen, it will be my treat. C'mon." I pulled out my ace. "It's your weekend off anyway, so a few extra hours on Cassie will be good for her. I'll even let you pick the restaurant. Please?"

"Dalton would admire your stubbornness! If Dianne agrees then, yes, dinner would be a nice change. Cassie's just come inside now, so I'll go and ask her."

"Excellent. Don't ask her - tell her."

***

Arriving home earlier than usual, I found Jan finishing up laundry. She greeted me with a smile. "I think it did Cassie good to have an unexpected change of plans for dinner, so now I can thank you for the break from the kitchen. I need to resist becoming someone who gets set in their ways."

I gave her a quick hug. "I know Cassie can be a bit flaky at times, especially with her creative meal ideas, but it might be helpful to give her more responsibility. And for the record, I don't see you as a person who would ever become set in their ways."

"Thank you. I guess time will tell. I did warn her about the pot smoking. Not to happen—ever—when she is in charge. By her guilty face, I may have mentioned it just in time."

We both laughed. Then I grew serious. "I am relieved you and Dianne will have dinner with me. I expect I have some venting to do."

Her eyes, so full of wisdom and care, almost brought me to another round of tears. I swiped one hand across my cheek. "Back to Cassie. I know, at times, you have qualms over her abilities, but she'll be fine."

"You're right, little one. I'll try. Now, you said I could pick the restaurant? How about the Rivermill? I've heard glowing reports about the seafood choices."

"Perfect. Oh, but we might need reservations."

"Well, I took the liberty..."

"What time?"

"For six-thirty. I wasn't sure you'd be home early, but now you've lots of time to freshen up." Jan looked down at her apron and work clothes. "I doubt these would be acceptable at the Rivermill, so I'd best find something suitable."

I knew Dianne would clean up well, and I had an idea of what I'd choose. "We had such a good time at the spa last month, didn't we? Time for the three amigos to put our mark on the restaurant!"

Jan's face brightened. "Oh, yes what a fun day. Better than I thought. Now, shoo. Let me finish up here so I can get ready. You might want to find Dianne and give her the details. Oh, and I volunteer to be the DD if you like? That way you and Dianne can enjoy whatever fancy cocktails are being offered."

I planted a kiss on her cheek and set out to find Dianne.

***

Dianne had gone into town, so I texted her with the details. She agreed to be back on time.

I went upstairs contemplating how a long soak in the tub would be the best start to the evening. As I wandered around the apartment, sadness crept in. How fast life can change. It wouldn't be the same here without him and I grieved over what might have been. But then my pragmatic side took over. Deep down, I questioned if I hadn't been aware on some level that our relationship had run its course.

***

We pulled into the Rivermill parking lot and Jan reiterated she was happy to do the driving. "I'm okay with a drink now and then, but honestly, I prefer it to be in my home. I've seen too much in my life around the damage alcohol can do. But don't let my musings spoil our evening."

"Oh, you won't." Dianne and I spoke at the same time. The evening was off to a pleasant start, morale positive, and once Jan handed off the car for valet parking, we made our way inside.

Dianne tried to act surprised at the compliments we gave her on her glamorous threads. "Oh, this? It doesn't get much mileage in these parts, so I shook off the moths and decided to give it a run one last time. Or do you think it's too much bling for this place?"

"Dianne, rest assured - you set the standard." Jan laughed in a good-natured way.

And then we stopped speaking to take in our surroundings. Some of the brick from the old mill had been kept as a feature wall. Framed sketches played out scenes from the history of Grant's Crossing. Quite a few of the homes and buildings shown still existed.

Subdued music added to the atmosphere of tranquillity and refinement. The dining room buzzed with diners and staff. Crisp white linen cloths and sparkling glassware invited us in.

Dianne spoke in a whisper. "Wow, they know how to do things in style here."

"And you worried about fitting in." I gave her a slight elbow jab as the hostess settled us at an immaculately set table, near a window. The view told me we were atop the old water wheel, and we could look down on the Alder River below. Across the river, car lights began to twinkle as daylight slipped away.

"Your server this evening will be Tiffany and she'll be with you shortly. Enjoy."

Once the hostess left us, Jan leaned in across the table. "I dropped the Grant name when making the reservation. There should be some perks to being the great granddaughter of the original owner."

"Well played, Jan! I really like what they've done to this place. No resemblance to the time I was held captive here last year. It's a distant memory now." Why did I say that? What a way to put a damper on the evening. I changed course. "Lots more to consider without dwelling on the past."

Jan patted my hand. "That's a healthy attitude."

A young girl, smartly dressed in black pants and a starched white blouse approached. Had to be Tiffany, and she requested our drinks order. I deferred to Dianne. "How about you order for us?"

"Happy to. We'll have two vodka martinis and a club soda, please."

Tiffany bobbed her head and left to oblige us. We made small talk until the drinks were in front of us, then I proposed a toast. "Here's to us, ladies. To cherished friends and shared experiences - the good and the bad."

We touched our glasses, took a sip, and then I grew serious. "I'm glad we're here, away from ears and eyes, if you know what I mean. In case you didn't know it, I'm counting on you both for your wisdom to help me through these changes I find myself dealing with."

Jan spoke to me. "Little one, this was a fine idea to talk away from the lodge. And before you ask, I have made it clear to Cassie that there is to be no mudslinging around you and Jeff. I can't control the others so much though. I suggested to Cassie it might be a good evening for some board games or cards. A perfect way to keep them busy."

"Maybe the Monopoly board will get a workout! Don't worry about the gossip, Jan. It's bound to happen. Even Bennett already knows about it." I recapped my talk with him for them both. Finishing with my guess that he and Nina would soon be more than friends.

"Wonders will never cease. Although, by all accounts they are a good match." Jan looked about to say more but Tiffany had returned to take our food orders.

Jan and I ordered trout, while Dianne opted for a beef wellington. While we waited, Jan came back with a question. "Will Jeff continue working with the alpacas?"

For the next while, interrupted only by our meals arriving, I brought my dinner companions up to date. The whole she-bang from our time at university to our arrival in Grant's Crossing. How at first, we were happy to settle in, but over the months cracks had begun to appear. Small at first, but then larger and larger.

They let me vent and when I had exhausted the story, it left me drained, but somehow elated. Maybe elated's not the right word, but I felt more optimistic about my future without Jeff. That's when I knew I would be alright.

To give them both credit, they waited for me to ask their opinion, before offering unsolicited advice. Dianne spoke first.

"My friend, you know my track record with relationships, so I may not be the expert you need. When things go wrong, we tend to lay blame on the other, but it takes two - whether to make it or break it. In this case, I think you've outgrown Jeff. Some things are not meant to be. Let him go and wish him well. You will always be friends. You're young but have a smart and mature head on your shoulders, so work at your career goals and enjoy your life here if it's what you want. You are going to be okay. You're stronger than you give yourself credit for."

I don't know what I expected from Dianne, but it wasn't this. I assumed she'd be angry at Jeff and tell me all sorts of things. Like it's time to have some fun and play the field etcetera. I guess I have a lot to learn about relationships. And more to learn about her as well.

I turned to Jan. "I know how fond of Jeff you are. Please tell me what you think."

Her gaze fell on both of us in turn. "Alysha, you know about my past with Dalton, and why I never married. I agree with what Dianne has said and you'll get through this. You are a resilient and independent woman. I don't believe you need our advice. Yes, I care for Jeff and that won't change. But you are in my heart, and I will always be here for you."

I thought my heart would burst with the love and admiration I felt for these two important women in my life. Any pent-up tension I had been feeling evaporated. Yes, I would be fine.

I reached for the dessert menu. "Right, who's having cake?"

CHAPTER FOURTEEN

Dianne

Another overcast day, but at least the rain had stopped. I didn't have much on tap to occupy myself. Might be the day to take Minnie for a drive. Yes, and by that, I mean get it out of the way. I did offer.

They say a leopard can't change its spots; well, they've never met Minnie Parker. No way I'd have seen this complete character change coming a year ago. To be honest, sometimes I missed the abrasive side of her. In the past a lot of mealtimes saw me biting my tongue and anticipating colourful exchanges around the dinner table. No one had been immune to her acerbic attacks. Other than Jan. Minnie rarely lashed out at her. Not wise to bite the hand that feeds you.

Frank had been a tremendous help with her when she finally crashed. Learning her back story, their romance and marriage that never happened, helped us see her in a different light. To me, though the fact she and Sasitha hit it off underscored how much she'd changed.

What the heck. I enjoyed driving. She might welcome a break from Rose and Lily. Those two were all over her since she'd come home. Suffocating, more like. At least with Sasitha they'd developed a mutual friendship. Rose saw Minnie as a makeover project and Lily tagged along for the ride.

I knocked on Minnie's door. When she opened it, I instinctively flinched; old habits die hard. But she was pleasant. "Can I help you, Dianne?"

I peered over her shoulder and could see she'd been knitting. Her decades-old habit hadn't left, but now she had a focus for her needles and yarn. Not only had she volunteered to knit hats and mitts for a social services agency but had decided to participate in the knitted crafts event at the Fall Fair. And I guess I was surprised to see her room clean and orderly. Not that long ago, she'd been a hoarder. Mostly of food pilfered from our meals.

"I, uh, wondered if you might like to get out for a bit. Go for a drive? We could stop for lunch somewhere." Oh, frig, I hadn't meant to go that far.

Her eyes narrowed to match the tightness of her lips. I began to regret my altruistic overture. "But if you're busy, we can do it another time." I started to back away when her claw-like hand grabbed my wrist.

"What a lovely idea. I had wanted Frank to take me into town, but he can't today. I need to go to the market – can we do that?"

Oh no. The market. Where I hadn't shown my face since the shoving match. Well, since no one put me in this corner but me, what could I say. "Glad to, Minnie. If you need time to get ready...?"

"Ten minutes. I'll meet you downstairs." I still found her smile a little unnatural. But maybe she was getting used to it as well. Her former perpetual scowl had only highlighted the lines and wrinkles on her face. The smile did take a few years off. Thank goodness, she wasn't prone to the garish makeup Rose and Lily preferred. So far, it would appear, Rose hadn't made a similar improvement with Minnie.

***

I declined to enter the market with her and waited outside in the car. She soon joined me and put two bags of items in the back. "Where are we heading?"

I didn't have a specific destination, other than a roadside café about an hour away. "Have you ever eaten at The Fox's Den? I've been there a couple of times."

She buckled her seat belt. "No, but Frank's mentioned it. Too bad most of the trees have lost their leaves. It would be a pretty drive."

And we were off. Awkward silences aren't my thing, but I realized I didn't know what to say, other than trite small talk. "How's the knitting?"

She proceeded to describe various patterns and varieties of wool which meant nothing to me, but I let her run with it. Then the silence returned.

We were about halfway to our destination when I slowed and pulled to the right-hand side of the road. An ambulance and police cruiser screamed past us.

"Someone's in trouble," I commented. I kept my eyes on the disappearing lights, until they pulled into the parking lot of a touristy motel not far ahead. Well, who wouldn't be curious, so I slowed right down. My foot hit the brake when I saw Sherri Wallis outside one of the motel doors.

"Hang on Minnie. Change of plans." I pulled into the far end of the parking lot, shut the engine off and watched.

"What's going on, Dianne? You can't be that nosey!" Aha! A slight hint of old Minnie, but I didn't react.

"Sorry. See that woman standing over there talking to the police?" I pointed to Sherri, who stood with her coat pulled tightly around here. The wind tossed her long hair around her face. And even from where I sat, the dark circles under her eyes stood out in her pale face. Her head swivelled between the officer and the door to one of the motel units. "I know her. Had coffee with her yesterday."

And then I saw the pick-up truck with Brodan Contracting lettered on its door. Had her husband been found? "Oh crap, I hope nothing's happened to her husband."

"How do you know this person? Are we going to be here long? You did say we'd be eating."

I couldn't risk a full-blown return of the old Minnie. "We won't stop long, promise. I'm just concerned for my friend, you know?"

She relaxed back into the seat and mumbled, "Seeing as I'm a captive audience, I don't have much choice but to wait."

"Have you taken your meds today?" Damn, no control over my inside voice today.

She answered with an exasperated sigh, and then pointed to where Sherri stood. "Look."

The motel room door opened, and a paramedic backed out of the room, pulling on a gurney to get it out the doorway. The wail I heard from Sherri pierced my guts and I watched in silence as she collapsed to her knees. The gurney held a head-to-toe covered body, but it had to be Brock Wallis.

***

An hour later, Minnie and I sat at a table in The Fox's Den. She had a healthy appetite, but I could only push the French fries around on my plate. I couldn't shake the image of Sherri Wallis being comforted by a police officer. I was anxious to get back home, but Minnie refused to be rushed. She wouldn't leave without a piece of apple pie.

I downed another coffee and stewed. Resentment over all things Minnie bubbled in my throat. If I didn't get her home soon, the paramedics would have another patient. And it wouldn't be me!

She still knew how to push the buttons - maybe some of those leopard spots were imitation.

My phone vibrated in my purse. Alysha's name appeared on the screen. I hoped she'd provide an excuse for us to get back on the road.

"Hi Alysha...what's up?"

The excuse she supplied wasn't what I'd expected.

"Jeff's been picked up by Dubois. His fingerprints are all over the murder weapon!"

CHAPTER FIFTEEN

Alysha

When DC Dubois had called—as a courtesy to me—to say Jeff had been arrested under suspicion of murder in April Lancashire's death, he didn't know Jeff was technically no longer my problem. At first, I couldn't understand how they would have his prints, but then I remembered. Back when we were at university, Jeff had worked with computer security, requiring a police check and provided his prints at the time.

What am I saying! Of course, he's my problem. Despite what's happened, and how much he's let me down, I still care for him. I know he'd never hurt a fly. I had let Steven Dubois be party to my sentiments in short order.

I punched at a pillow on the sofa and wanted to scream in frustration - and fear. There had to have been a mistake, a distortion of facts. Surely there'd be a suitable explanation for this mess! Dubois had it wrong once before, with Dianne, and Jackson's murder in the summer. It could happen again, couldn't it?

I needed to talk to someone.

It was Jan's weekend off and there's no way I'd ever confide in Cassie. Besides, she has enough to deal with when Jan's away.

I pulled on a hoodie and went downstairs to the next level and knocked on Dianne's door. When she didn't respond I opened my phone and called to see where she was.

"Are you nearby? Something awful has happened here, and I could use someone to talk to."

"Is someone hurt? Are you okay?"

"It's not me. Jeff's been picked up by Dubois. His fingerprints are all over the murder weapon!"

"What! Listen, I'm about half an hour away from home and am heading back now. Hang tight till I get there, okay?"

I could only mumble a response. Anxiety had gripped my heart and left me tongue-tied.

"Not been a stellar day for me either, but Jeff being arrested takes the cake. I'll be there soon as I can."

She didn't provide details on her news, but to be honest, I didn't much care. Her voice was strained when I heard her speak to someone close by, "We have to go now."

Then her voice returned to me. "It will be okay, Alysha. Remember to breathe."

"Thanks, Dianne. Drive safe, please. The police have been busy enough for one day without handing out speeding tickets."

"Alysha, you have no idea. See you soon."

And with that cryptic remark, the call ended leaving me with no one else I could talk to I longed for the reassurance of my friends to tell me I wasn't dreaming.

I grabbed a broom from the kitchen and headed out to the veranda to wait on Dianne. Nobody else was about and sweeping up leaves gave me an excuse to burn off my anxieties.

Dry leaves scattered in advance of my rigorous onslaught as I rehearsed my request to have Dianne come with me to the police station. I stood back to admire my efforts when I heard car tires crunch on the gravel driveway.

Dianne. Finally, thank heavens. She had a passenger, too. Minnie?

Occupied with helping her out of the car, she hadn't yet noticed me.

Her apology-laced tone to Minnie resulted in a grunt. "Now, Minnie, I'm sorry our day was cut short, but I know you'll understand Alysha's urgent message gave me no choice. I promise to make it up to you another day. Preferably when the sun is shining as well."

Minnie shot Dianne one of her old grimaces, but then replaced it with an understanding smile. "Never mind, Dianne. I enjoyed getting out for a bit of fresh air." She nodded at me in passing and touched my shoulder. "Whatever the problem is, Alysha, I'm sure things will work out."

Once the front door closed behind her, I spoke to Dianne. "I'm sorry for interrupting your drive. I wasn't aware you were out with Minnie. Was that your idea? Nice of you." Inane rambling tended to be my curse when stressed. I managed one clear question. "Nothing's wrong with Minnie I hope?"

Dianne's brow knitted over eyes full of concern, as she tossed her keys into her purse. She released a deep sigh.

"Never mind Minnie, she's fine." Dianne kept talking as she moved us indoors where it was warmer. After peeking into the media room and ensuring it was empty, we went in. She stood face to face with me. "Right, I do have a story for you, but it can wait. Why the hell has Jeff been arrested?"

Damn. I was afraid of this. I fought back tears, threatening to spill. I wouldn't cry... I wouldn't! Taking a deep breath, I made my request. "Can I ask if you'd go to the police station with me. I need to find out for myself what's going on. Would you mind - going now?"

Pulling her car keys back out, she said, "Not at all. What are friends for? I don't for a minute believe Jeff had anything to do with this murder. He'd never hurt anyone. C'mon. While I drive, I'll give you the condensed version of what I saw this afternoon; might be a worthy distraction for a few minutes. Let's go!"

Dianne took control, and true to her word she gave me a rundown of her meeting yesterday with Sherri Wallis and then the outcome at the motel this afternoon.

"Wow. Will you have a chance to talk with her again? You should tell Dubois what she told you. Right, Dianne?"

"I know. But I'd be breaking a confidence."

"Besides you don't need to be charged with obstructing justice, or something, do you? As her friend, let her know you didn't want to, but you had no choice. Remember, it's Jeff we're talking about here. I refuse to believe he's involved!" I realized I hoped to shift blame from Jeff to Sherri's husband. Did that make me a terrible person?

"But didn't you say his fingerprints were on the murder weapon?"

That silenced me and I wrestled with my thoughts, as we parked outside the storefront location of the Grant's Crossing's police station.

My hand hesitated on the car door handle because I had second thoughts about going in. I'd just seen my nemesis exit her car and head inside. I pointed her out to Dianne. "That's Gillian."

"So? Doesn't matter. What are we waiting for, Alysha? We have business here." Dianne offered me a comforting smile. "I'll be getting a reputation for visiting the cop shop too often. But you're right. I need to tell what I know. I only hope Sherri will understand how the police depend on all the facts to get to the truth."

***

The police substation was compact in space, and crowded, which meant I stood behind Gillian Walker, in line waiting to get answers.

No surprise she'd arrived here to see about Jeff, also. I should have been better than this, but I checked her out from top to toe. Would she sense my appraisal as I scrutinized her, hoping to find a flaw, or impediment? I could see Jeff's attraction to her. She's everything I'm not. Did I mention gorgeous? Tall and slim. Rural chic, right down to her signature Wellington boots. And she loves alpacas. Was that the defining attraction? I'd swear Jeff never had a wandering eye all the time we were together. But someone who shares his love of our woolly friends, well, that must have clinched the deal.

I gave myself a shake—annoyed my thoughts could so easily drift from what was important—as we inched closer to the information desk. Gillian had moved away. Her only acknowledgement of me was a tight smile.

I stood before the new officer I'd met at the lodge the other day. He closed a file folder and looked up at me. "How may I help you? Oh, hi Ms. Grant. Are you here to see DC Dubois?"

"Constable Truman, isn't it? No, not Dubois, yet. I believe you're holding Jeff Iverson here. I need to see him!"

Truman's expression held no smile when he addressed me. "I'm sorry. Like I told the other lady, Mr. Iverson's being processed at the moment. No visitors allowed right now. I can see if DC Dubois will see you, after he speaks with Ms. Walker?"

This wasn't going as planned and my mind refused to give me options. Dianne took over.

"Listen, see the thing is... We, that is I, might have some information pertinent to the murder. It could affect Jeff's arrest. So, it's connected. And can't wait!"

I mentally blessed Dianne for her confidence and ability to say what I should have. But Truman remained annoyingly slow to respond. What was wrong with him!

He finished writing a comment on the paper in front of him and calmly said, "I'll inform Dubois you're here. But, be warned, you might have a long wait."

Not what I wanted to hear; my primary concern was Jeff. Dianne held me in check. "He's just doing his job."

I got it and tried to remain civil. "We'll wait, then, as long as it takes. Do I need to get Jeff a lawyer?"

Truman stayed all business and not to be put off his script. "It's best you speak to DC Dubois first. You see, Ms. Walker has already offered to arrange a lawyer for him, if needed." Truman indicated Gillian Walker who now sat in the tiny waiting room, staring at the floor.

Dianne pulled at my elbow. "Let's grab a seat. Lucky there's two left."

I didn't mean to whine, but that's how it sounded. "I really need to see Jeff." Likely a useless plea, but I said it anyway.

My hopes were dashed when Truman didn't move from his post, and merely offered a small shrug of his shoulders.

Dianne and I took the remaining seats in the waiting room. She took out her cell phone and left me to consider the absurdity of sitting next to Gillian in this cramped waiting room. We turned to look at each other at the same time. Tears streaked her face.

Oh, brother! How many times had I told Dianne to take the higher road and now I had to eat those words. My weak words of intended comfort mixed with commiseration, flowed faster than her tears. She had to be freaked out, like me.

"Gillian, we all know Jeff is innocent. In fact, Dianne, and I, oh, this is Dianne Mitchell, she also lives at the lodge. Well, she has some important information that may have a bearing on what's happened." Even to my own ears, I knew I babbled. I told myself to shut up before I said something truly embarrassing.

Gillian nodded at Dianne, then blew her nose, wiping tears away as she worked to compose herself. "I want so hard to believe he's innocent." She peered at me. "You certainly know him better than me, but I can't for a moment believe he's involved. He has no motive for killing a woman he doesn't know well. I was with him when DC Dubois arrested him. Jeff asked me to find a lawyer. Just in case. But then I think, what about the fingerprints on the weapon, a piece of wood? His prints would have been all over the lumber used for the stage sets, right? Jeff told me he'd dropped off quite a bit the last couple of weeks for props and things. Damn, I wish he'd never been involved with them in the first place."

Gillian had run out of steam and slumped down as far as the plastic chair would allow. The tears were threatening again so I handed her some clean tissue from my purse. I could see her genuine concern, and care, for Jeff. With some reluctance I knew I had to surrender when I concluded she was better a friend than an enemy.

Truman's voice intruded. "Gillian Walker? You can see DC Dubois now. I'll take you to him."

That stung, but to be fair, she had been here ahead of me. Looked like it would be Dubois only after Gillian went first

Gillian hesitated, and then stood. Her downcast expression seemed to ask how the hell she found herself here, as she followed Truman.

Time came to a standstill. Each time I glanced at the oversized clock on the wall, it didn't seem to move. Dianne and I had exhausted small talk. On some level I knew I should talk to her about what she'd seen earlier, but I didn't have the energy.

Eventually, the door behind Truman opened and Gillian came through. Her eyes were puffy, and she barely glanced at us but hurried for the door. Truman crooked a finger at us.

"Ms. Grant, DC Dubois will see you both now. Through that corridor, he's waiting for you."

I followed Dianne's lead as we found our way to an interview room. My thoughts wouldn't leave Jeff and I agonized over where he was in this place. He must be so scared.

Dubois greeted us as we came into another undersized room. "Take a seat, Alysha. And Ms. Mitchell."

Our chairs scraped across the concrete floor as we settled ourselves. Dubois tapped his pen on the institutional metal table we sat at. "I understand the reason for Alysha being here, but do you have a specific reason, Ms. Mitchell?"

I rushed to beat Dianne to the punch. "We're both here for the same reason, or should I say, person. And while I'm anxious to see Jeff— he shouldn't be here!—what Dianne has to tell you may give you another lead on the murder."

He smoothed a fresh sheet of paper and poised his pen. "I'm listening. How about we start with you, then, Ms Mitchell."

Dianne's prior history with the police didn't bode well for how she'd respond, but this was her information to tell. I prayed she'd stay polite.

She clasped her hands in front of her and drew a deliberate breath. "And good afternoon to you too, DC Dubois. I'm sure you know this is not my favourite place, especially after my experience a few months ago."

C'mon, Dianne. Keep cool. I pushed my thoughts her way, relieved when she relaxed her hands and raised the temperature of her voice a few degrees.

"However, if what I have to tell you means I help my friends then it will be worth it."

"And what, exactly, do you have to tell us regarding the death of April Lancashire?"

"First let me say, I'm betraying a trust and I can't verify what I've heard. But you can be the judge of whether it's important or not."

Dubois didn't respond. I recognized the tactic. Stay silent and the interviewee will spill their guts. I've read too many police procedurals. But it worked. She began to recount her meeting with Sherri. The concern Sherri had about her husband, Brock, and her worry that he somehow might be involved with the murder at the theatre.

My hands were clenched so tightly in my lap, they'd gone cold. I flexed them to get the circulation going again and tried to concentrate on what Dianne was saying.

"And when I happened on the scene at the motel earlier today... Well, it rattled me. And I guess, it means betraying a confidence is no longer a point. I assume the provincial police have informed you that Sherri Wallis is now a widow. I mean, if it's been confirmed the body I saw removed was her husband?"

She leaned back in the chair, and I patted her arm. But she wasn't quite finished. "For the record, my money is not on Jeff Iverson being involved. No matter what evidence you may have."

Dubois made no comment; the room fell silent other than the buzzing from the overhead fluorescent light. I forced my tense shoulders to drop. "Will I be able to see Jeff? He must be upset and..."

Dubois ignored my request and stayed focused on Dianne. "Ms. Mitchell. This information may be useful, thank you. I will check with our provincial police counterparts to confirm what you've told us." Then he looked at me. "As for Jeff, once this information is integrated into our investigation it may have bearing on his status with us. You are aware we have his fingerprints on the piece of lumber identified as the murder weapon?"

"Yes," I said. "But can I see him? I need to know he's alright."

"He softened his tone. "Listen, Alysha. I know this is hard, and these things often move at a snail's pace, but let me assure you, Jeff is fine. He's been cooperative, which goes a long way in his favour should this end up going to trial."

What the hell? Talk about mixed messages. Do they think he's guilty or not?

"Try not to worry, alright?" Dubois began gathering his papers. "We're done for now and I thank you both for coming in. Now, Alysha, if you'd like to see Jeff, it can be arranged."

"Does he need a lawyer? Gillian mentioned she'd get one if need be."

"Calling a lawyer is his choice, and I won't comment either way."

Dianne had a question I hadn't thought of. "Are there any other suspects, then?"

Dubois' face matched the lack of expression in his voice. "Sorry, not at liberty to say."

Big help there. "Can I see him now?"

"Yes, of course. It's just down the hall." He put an arm out in front of Dianne. "Sorry, only one allowed, you'll need to return to the waiting area. Oh, and Alysha if Gillian is still there, you'll have to wait as well."

"She's left already. I saw her before we came in here." Small comfort I knew something Dubois didn't.

Dianne left and before Dubois and I took another step, he had a question. "Out of curiosity, why is this Gillian Walker so concerned about Jeff? Is this a new friendship? My partner tells me she's offered to get him a lawyer and was visibly upset in the waiting area. Any idea why?"

Let him find out by the usual grapevine like everybody else about my love life.

"It's complicated. Can you take me to see Jeff please?"

CHAPTER SIXTEEN

Dianne

What a day! I haven't had a minute to myself since heading out with Minnie earlier. Twenty-four hours ago, I'd never have predicted the day would see me taking her for a drive and then ending up with Alysha and me at the police station. I itched to contact Sherri Wallis, but Alysha and I had only just come back from town and Cassie impatiently informed us dinner was being held until we sat down!

I tossed my jacket onto my bed and made a quick visit to the bathroom to freshen up. Then I hustled down to the dining room. Alysha had just settled into her seat and a roomful of eyes turned my way.

Quick mental review before I said anything out of place. Minnie would have filled them in on the motel scene. Alysha had no time to talk about Jeff's arrest. But Minnie, again, knew something had been amiss when we got back home. Fortunately, Alysha and I had managed to plan what to say and what not to say at dinner.

I'd let her take the lead. But first, what on earth were we dining on tonight? Oh, no way. Please tell me that's not a jellied salad. Those things hadn't been popular in years. Too much gelatinous green with unidentifiable objects floating inside a Bundt-pan shape made me queasy. Minnie and Philip seemed happy with it. Sasitha and Bachan looked on in polite disbelief.

Cassie beamed as she explained. "I found an old cookbook of Estelle's. Apparently, these salads were like a mealtime epidemic in the fifties and sixties. Thought it might be fun to try one."

Sasitha wobbled a spoonful onto her plate. "Tell me dear Cassie. What, please, are these shapes?"

"There's celery and cucumber. And the white little things are marshmallows. Some people say this should be more of a dessert, but I thought it might be okay for a side salad. Enjoy. I'll bring out the roast chicken in just a sec!"

Alysha wrinkled her nose. "I vaguely remember Gran making these. I think there was a horrible one made with salmon." And then Alysha backpedalled a bit. "But please everyone, for Cassie's sake, give it a try?"

The salad made for a worthy diversion, and not until most of the chicken and rice had disappeared did conversation finally come around to the day's events. Minnie of all people, trying out her new social skills, started the ball rolling.

"Alysha. I hope things will be alright for you. You were upset when Dianne and I drove up. Oh, and again, Dianne, thank you for the interesting day."

Alysha laid her knife and fork across her plate. Here we go. "Yes, Minnie. Thank you for asking. I guess most of you know ..."

She stopped mid-sentence, turning to me for reassurance. I smiled. "We're all friends here, and we love you, too. Got it?"

She nodded and continued. "Right. You all know Jeff is no longer living here." She put up a hand. "Even though I know you all care, please don't ask me about it. I may feel like sharing at some point but not now."

Heads nodded around the table. Except for Philip. He'd opened one of his books and patiently read while waiting on dessert, or for the conversation to change. He probably didn't care which.

"This afternoon, Dianne and I went to the police station to see Jeff."

Cue Rose, throwing her hand to her throat and uttering a most theatrical gasp, which Alysha ignored.

"Some of you may have heard he's been arrested by the police concerning the death of April Lancashire. He's being helpful to them in their investigation. I don't for one minute believe he's involved."

"Was his new girlfriend there, too?"

Oh, brother. Cassie. Cassie bigmouth. She looked stunned when everyone stared at her after the comment, even as she distributed slices of cake around the table. "What? Who doesn't know he's with that new vet assistant, Gillian Walker?"

She put a slice of cake in front of me. I grasped her hand and stood up. "Can I have a word, please. In the kitchen. Now."

"It's okay, Dianne. Honestly. Sit back down." Alysha gave me a small smile and put on a brave face.

I complied, but not without first giving Cassie a hard stare. The penny must have dropped because her face blanched and her voice dropped to a whisper. "Oh crap. Jan will kill me! She told me not to say anything, but I thought everyone knew, and..."

Sasitha had risen from the table and stood behind Cassie. "Now, dear girl, do not worry so. Let us both be going to the kitchen, and I will help with bringing out the tea and the coffee, yes?"

Without another word, Sasitha put her hand on Cassie's shoulder and guided her back to the kitchen. Another Kodak moment for Leven Lodge. Alysha opened her mouth to speak, when the front door flew open, and Nina arrived, sashaying into the dining room. "Hello all you foodies. Am I late for dinner? Oh. Cake!"

A dependable icebreaker is our Nina.

"Is Hemingway with you?" asked Lily, her eyes bright with anticipation.

"No, sorry, sunshine. I've left my precious with Bennett for an hour or two. They need some bonding time. Thought I'd stop by for dinner and a catch-up, but I'd say I've missed all the fun. What's new with all of you?"

"Jeff's only been arrested, that's all," blurted Rose. "But then if you were here more often, you'd be in the loop."

Oh, for crying out loud, Rose. Give it a rest. I tried damage control. "Nina, listen. He's been arrested, but we know it's been a mistake. I can fill you in later. No need to rehash old news in front of Alysha - if you get my drift?"

Nina, thank God, was savvy and didn't take Rose's bait. I relaxed a bit and went on the offensive to deflect from Alysha. "It's been kind of a busy day around here, Nina. Have a piece of cake while I tell you what I saw today."

The spotlight stayed on me for a few minutes, giving Alysha time to regroup. "I took Minnie for a drive, and we planned to be out for most of the day. But before we could stop for lunch, we drove past a disturbing scene at a small motel." Okay, so I paused for effect, what the heck.

"Minnie told us all about it!" exclaimed Rose.

"And now we should much like to hear this in your very own words." Bachan's calm manner took the wind out of Rose's sails but didn't dampen Nina's curiosity.

"Some of you know the name of the contractor responsible for the theatre renovation. Brock Wallis."

"Is he the murderer?"

"Let Diane finish, Rose," Nina said, between mouthfuls of cake. Nina had Rose's number, thank goodness.

"We don't know who the murderer is, and neither do the cops!" I made eye contact with everyone but Philip and hoped they got the message. It's not Jeff!

"Anyway, I know Sherri Wallis a little bit and when I saw her with the police, I pulled into the parking lot. And then they brought out a body. All covered up, but I'm pretty sure it was her husband. She collapsed at the scene."

"And then we went for lunch," said Minnie in such a matter-of-fact tone, I nearly laughed.

"Yes, we did. I didn't think it proper to hang around the scene, although I hope to talk with Sherri tomorrow and see if I can find out what happened."

"So, another delay for the theatre renovation?" Philip had raised his head. Maybe he can read and listen at the same time. "The boarding passes will be out of date before the play sails."

"Sure, okay, Philip." Never question, just accept.

I fielded a few more questions, but the well of speculation had run dry and eventually everyone left the table, except Alysha and me.

"You doing okay, kiddo?"

"Right now, I don't know if I'll sleep from exhaustion or lie awake all night worrying. Thanks for steering the conversation away from Jeff. You did it well."

"Hey, we're a team, right. If Jan had been here, the three amigos would have had them all running for the hills!" It made me happy to see her break a smile and I was about to say more when a commotion from the kitchen drew our attention.

Cassie's raised voice had me alarmed, but who was she talking to?

We both entered the kitchen where Cassie, red-faced, was in a heated conversation with her friend from the bookstore. "Griffith Sharples," I whispered to Alysha.

She moved ahead of me. "Everything alright here, Cassie?"

"Sorry, Alysha. I didn't mean to disturb you. Griff is just leaving. He's not fond of the word no."

"What's happening? Did Cassie invite you here, Griff?" Alysha's manner put her in charge. Her home, her staff, her way.

In contrast to Cassie's flustered state, Griff sported a woebegone expression. Up close this time, I got a look at puppy-dog eyes in a boyish face. In a flash, his face brightened with a sunny smile, and he turned his charm on Alysha. "No, she didn't exactly. See, I keep asking her out, but she always says she's so busy working here, or at the tavern. So, I thought I'd come by and see if I could catch her on a break or something. You're her boss, right? What do you say, can she stop work early?"

Cassie rolled her eyes. "Griff, please, I like you, but I don't want to go out with you."

"Hey, you're involved with the Countryside Players, aren't you? Did you know April Lancashire?" I seized an opportunity to gather information.

His face fell. "Sort of. That is, I've had a few minor parts with them, and keep trying to get a bigger role. So, I kind of knew her a little."

I pressed on. "When was the last time you saw her?"

He cocked his head. "Hmmm. Can't remember exactly. What I do remember is she'd been talking with Kyle Foreman. He's a playwright, you know. Anyway, she talked, he screamed. Accused her of taking the play from some new playwright who plagiarized one of his plays. Boy, talk about steamed. But she was pretty cool. Told him she'd check with Matthew Fielding and get back to him."

"And Matthew Fielding is who?" asked Alysha.

"Oh, right. Sorry. Matthew Fielding. He wrote the new play that's supposed to be for the opening. Boy, Kyle Foreman hates his guts. Never saw someone so angry."

Despite the seriousness of the conversation he relayed to us, he only had moon-eyes for Cassie. The tone of his voice didn't line up with what he told us. Even for Cassie, this guy was a bit too much, no big surprise she tried to put him off. I had a nickname for this guy – Sunny Jim, or Simple Simon. I bet pigeon poop wouldn't stick on him. Sheesh!

Alysha moved a little closer to him. "Okay, Griff? It's time to call it a night. Cassie is *not* finishing her shift early. And you might want to share this information with the police. They're interested in anyone who might have had a grudge with April." Alysha tried the subtle approach. I had a feeling it wouldn't work.

"She's right, Griff." Cassie tried a placating tone. "Remember, they thought you were upset with her and suspicious of you a little? This is way worse."

"Gosh. Maybe you're right. Okay. I'll be on my way. Can I call you tomorrow, Cassie, after I talk to the police?"

Cassie exhaled. "If you must. But I'm not going out with you. Got it!"

He only smiled. "I'll keep trying to convince you. Goodnight, all."

The back door closed on Griffith and his tuneless whistling. Cassie threw a tea towel over her shoulder and went back to cleaning up the kitchen. Out of sight, out of mind.

Alysha and I left the kitchen and walked to the bottom of the stairs. We both let out pent-up, and much needed, giggles we'd kept from Cassie. Talk about a day of extremes.

"I don't even want to think about tomorrow right now. Time for a soak in the tub and then head to bed."

"Sounds like comforting medicine, Alysha. I'm ready to call it a day as well. Who knows what tomorrow will bring?"

We started up the stairs when Alysha's cell phone rang. She looked at the screen, then at me. "It's Gillian."

CHAPTER SEVENTEEN

Alysha

I held the phone away from my ear and said goodnight to Dianne. I'm sure she would have preferred to listen in, but she got the hint and moved away I went back to the call. "Gillian?"

"Hi, Alysha. I hope you don't mind me calling this late, but I've managed to secure a lawyer for Jeff, and he'll visit tomorrow. I, um, I'll help Jeff with the legal fees."

I had well and truly been replaced. The realization cut deep, but I'd give in to the emotion of it later. For now, I stayed cool. "No problem. He's a criminal lawyer - the one you've hired?"

"The clinic has used him from time to time, and he has had experience with criminal law. For now, I believe, his priority is to see about bail, assuming the judge grants it."

And she has legal experience to boot. I swallowed hard. "I appreciate all you're doing... Listen, I'll give you guys some space, but you do know Jeff has been a big part of my life, so this is not easy for me. Please update me regarding the lawyer. I can help with the bail money if needed. But from here on in, he's your baby." I paused to take a breath. "I don't need to tell you I believe in his innocence. Jeff doesn't have a mean bone in his body. There is no way, ever, he could be a murderer!"

There was momentary silence on the other end after my outburst, and then Gillian spoke - in a kinder tone than I deserved. "Alysha. I'm not insensitive to your history with Jeff, which puts us on the same page. So of course, I will keep you updated. And it goes without saying, I can always check in on the cria we were helping. While Jeff is... otherwise unavailable."

How civilized she sounds, still offering her services when she's taken my place with someone I thought I'd spend my life with. It appears I'm redundant. Well, I could be civilized, too. "We do have others capable of caring for the alpacas but if you think Ryker still needs veterinary attention then be my guest."

"Thank you, I'll be in touch."

I had no desire to be bosom buddies with Jeff's new amour, so I ended the call before I completely lost it.

My heart grew heavy, fuelled by a range of emotions I dared not give in to. I continued up the stairs to my oasis. Opening the door, I surveyed the apartment I'd shared with Jeff since coming to Grant's Crossing more than a year ago. I dwelt on how to move forward with the changes to my personal life. Time to take stock. I had friends here at the Lodge, and in town. Plus, I'd begun carving myself a career in real estate. The rooms at the top of the farmhouse had once belonged to my Uncle Dalton and was where I felt most at home. I'd always be grateful to him for this unexpected inheritance I now called home.

All I could ever need was right here and with that understanding came a burst of energy. I looked around. I'd need to leave no question this oasis belonged to me, and me alone.

Right! I'd need to clear out the rest of Jeff's things before the apartment could truly become mine. I didn't have any boxes, so I stuffed his clothes and belongings into garbage bags. His guitar, books, computer gadgets and his toiletries he could pick up once he's free. It might be better to be scarce when that happens. My cleaning accomplished, exhaustion overcame me, so I readied myself for bed. I made chamomile tea to help me sleep. My thoughts ricocheted all over the place, but they eventually settled on Jeff. I reflected on my visit with him earlier. A visit that hadn't lasted long.

My mind's eye replayed what I'd seen when the door had opened on the room where Jeff had been detained. What a tiny, claustrophobic space. Jeff sat at a small table, his head resting on his arms. He'd looked up at me. I didn't know if the anguish and confusion on his face was for me, or for the situation he found himself in.

I was dismayed to find myself tongue-tied, not sure where to begin or what to ask, other than a lame, "How are you doing?"

He shrugged. I noticed his eyes were bloodshot and he'd bitten his nails to the point of bleeding. He didn't belong there! My throat tightened and tears pricked at my eyes.

"Thanks for coming, Aly. You didn't need to."

I lowered my eyes and then finally found my voice. "Truman, out front, tells me Gillian will take care of getting you a lawyer. Not that you'll need one other than to get bail, right?"

He sat up straighter. "You know I didn't do this, don't you?"

I sat in the chair across from him and reached for his hand. "You don't even need to ask. So, tell me, just what do the police have?"

He explained the police had found his fingerprints on the plank of wood used in the murder. "But it's circumstantial. My fingerprints are on anything to do with stage sets because, as you know, I've been working on them for a while. The kicker is they want to know why my fingerprints are the only ones on the murder piece if I didn't do it. For crying out loud, have they never heard of wearing gloves!" His voice rose as he protested his innocence. He also let me know he'd overheard April argue with Brock Wallis, the contractor. He didn't want to interfere and said he left while they were still arguing. This jived with what Dianne had learned from Sherri about her husband. I reassured Jeff the police would realize his innocence.

Jeff turned sad eyes on me. "Dubois and the rest have to be on the ball with all this information, don't they?"

Now probably wasn't the best time to remark to Jeff, that I'd prefer Dax Young be on this case. I smiled in a non-committal way.

"I'm so relieved Gillian's found a lawyer for me. Fingers crossed this time tomorrow I'll be released, even if it's on bail." Gone were the sad eyes, replaced with a sparkle as he went on about Gillian this and Gillian that. Didn't take cupid to see he had it bad.

The man I'd once considered my life partner had become besotted with someone else. C'est la vie.

***

Heavy rain battered against my bedroom window, bringing me to a conscious state. I was surprised how well I'd slept. I stretched and kicked back the covers. A rumble of thunder confirmed there'd be no Sunday morning run today.

Sundays were normally free for me to do as I pleased as the Lodge pretty much ran itself, apart from mealtime. Jan was still away until evening, which meant another day of Cassie's cooking. I smirked to myself and vowed to stay clear of the kitchen and dining room. Just as well, because I had no wish to be questioned – or pitied.

After a quiet breakfast, I shot a text to Cassie to come up and see me, to go over the day's menu. Mealtime review was Jan's purview, but in her absence, I took over.

When Cassie arrived, I offered her a coffee, but she declined. Her excitement at describing the evening meal worried me. No doubt all of us would be subjected to one of her meal creations—or experiment—once again.

"Trust me, Alysha. I've got something special in mind for today's dinner. You're going to love it. It's a new recipe. Completely different!"

I hated to dampen her enthusiasm and had no stomach for uncharted culinary territory right now. "Cassie, please don't try any of your new concoctions while Jan is away."

She blew me off. "Don't you worry. It was Dianne who asked, and I obliged. I'm not telling you what it is. It's a surprise. And you're going to love the dessert as well. Guaranteed!"

I groaned inwardly, not letting on to my unease. She would have been oblivious even if I said anything because she blatantly scoured the room for any kind of dirt-dishing tidbit she could share with the rest of the house. When her eyes locked on the green garbage bags piled in a corner, I thought she might gasp aloud. Time to nip it in the bud, and I cut her off before she could start with the questions.

"Cassie. Cassie! You know I'm going through a personal situation right now and I want to keep it that way. Personal and private. When I've something to say concerning Jeff, I will let you, and the others, know, myself. Understood?"

Awesome! She looked properly chastised and apologized.

"Sorry, Alysha. It's just that, you know, we're all so worried about you both."

"I'll leave it up to you to reassure everyone I'm fine." I tried to get her to see how I felt. "Would you like it if I kept asking you questions about, what's his name, Griff? He comes across as super keen on you. But it's not my business, is it?"

"But I don't like him, and he keeps pestering me and..." She stopped when she saw the frustration on my face.

"Sorry Alysha, I get what you're saying". She smiled as she said, "My lips are sealed."

The girl seriously needs to grow up. "One more thing. I won't be down for dinner tonight so is there any chance you could leave me a plate of the surprise?"

"Will do. And some of my special dessert as well. Remember, once Jan is back, I'll be off for the rest of the evening. I'll be heading to the tavern to hang with my friends. Let's hope I don't bump into Griff."

I'd no more energy to respond because I don't think I even cared. Without another word she left, and I shook my head as the door closed behind her.

I spent the best part of the morning making lists and dealing with work-related paperwork. The rain had stopped, and a weak sun had appeared. Still too wet for a run so I rummaged in some boxes stashed in a cupboard space I'd reserved for all things relating to the Grants. It had become a day for reminiscing on family history but also looking forward. I'd make it a new beginning for me.

And then, I found what I had searched for. Dalton had kept copious notes on the history of the Grants. I hadn't looked at these papers since I'd first arrived. I reread about the Grants and my parents, taking comfort in the fact they were a family that understood a sense of community and always stayed the course. I knew then I'd be alright and would just take it one day at a time.

***

Cassie had done a thorough job of cleaning up the kitchen after dinner. This time of night most of the residents were settled in for the evening, and with luck I'd not run into any of them. After spending the afternoon shredding, sorting, and generally tidying up my clutter for a new start, I'd grown hungry and ready for my dinner. If Jan was in the kitchen, it would be a bonus for me.

Sitting at the kitchen table I demolished my dinner. I hadn't eaten since breakfast, and I would have to congratulate Cassie on her choice for a Sunday dinner. My fears had been unfounded; no mysterious greenery-loaded casserole this time. I assumed Cassie offered a vegetarian choice for the Patels—pretty sure they'd pass on the stuffed pork tenderloin—delicious as it was. Sasitha had been showing Cassie some meat-free curry dishes. I'd be happy to see those options as regular fare anytime!

The last forkful of seasoned, tender, meat left my plate and I sat back, sated. I became aware of the television blaring from the media room. That would be Rose and Lily. Might be time for a hearing check on those ladies, although Rose would be adamant nothing was wrong with *her* hearing! She'd probably attribute the hearing loss to Lily, and that she put up with the volume because that's the kind of long-suffering person she was. A situation Jan's best at handling, and I'd let her do so.

I was about to tackle a bowl of strawberry trifle left by Cassie when Jan came through the back door.

"Speak of the devil. I was just thinking about you."

"All good I hope." She began to unbutton her coat and placed her small overnight bag on the floor.

"Did you have a nice visit with your family?"

"I did, thank you. The time always goes by so fast." Her trademark smile filled her face, and she stood with her hands on her hips "Is there any left for me? Cassie can't go wrong with trifle unless she's put too much sherry in it?"

I scooped up a generous mouthful and let the flavours coat my tongue. "Yummy. No, no sherry this time but equally delicious." I pointed. "Check the fridge. She may have left you some. I'm glad you're back. I've so much to talk to you about."

***

I asked Jan to meet me in my apartment away from prying eyes and ears, after we'd finished our trifle, and left the kitchen clean.

"Give me twenty minutes to change into something comfy and shed my going-home-to-see-the-folk's persona. I may be nearly all talked out after answering endless questions by one and all about this murder in town. But I'll always have time for you, little one."

Jan's term of endearment for me never failed to lift my spirits. "Thanks. I'd ask Dianne, as well, but she went into town after dinner to meet a friend. Anyway, it's you I need to talk to."

Her face clouded. "Sounds ominous. Put the kettle on and we'll have a cup of tea. Then you can fill me in on what's happened."

True to her word she returned wearing a warm, fleece tracksuit and slippers. I recalled the first time she'd visited Jeff and me in the apartment. That time, she'd changed from her everyday housekeeper attire and wore clothing paying homage to her aboriginal status. That's when she told us stories of her long-term affair with my Uncle Dalton. She'd been a festival dancer when she met him and explained to us why they'd never married. One of the things I wanted to discuss with her tonight.

Sipping on her tea she sighed contentedly. "I feel so close to Dalton when I'm here. But I'm sure there are other things you want to talk about. Fill me in about Jeff."

For the next hour I recapped events that had happened after Jeff's arrest. What I'd learned from Dianne during her drive with Minnie and seeing Sherri Wallis' husband's body at the motel. I didn't dwell on Gillian except to say she'd found Jeff a lawyer.

She put her teacup down and didn't speak for a moment. "You've handled a lot this weekend. Perhaps I shouldn't go away so often because that's when all the excitement happens." Her teasing tone didn't hide the genuine caring in her voice. "But I'm here now and you're not on your own with things. Speaking of which - were there any problems here with our family or mealtimes?"

"I wouldn't say excitement, exactly."

"A little teasing, my friend, that's all. Don't lose your sense of humour when things are down, like Dalton always said."

"And Uncle Dalton was a wise man. He chose you, didn't he?"

Jan blushed, not something I'd seen often. "Now, Alysha, that's all in the past."

"And it's that past I want to talk to you about. I've spent today shedding my life with Jeff. I know it's over. I've had time to mull over what we discussed with you when we first came here. Remember? You shared the story of your life with Dalton. And the beautiful emerald and diamond ring that's been passed down through generations of Grants."

"I remember. You wanted me to keep it for you and Jeff if you married."

We gazed at each other, saddened by the turn of events.

"And it won't be happening now, Jan. So, please, keep it tucked away and don't be sending it to Jeff for Gillian!"

"As if I would." We both burst out giggling.

I agreed with Dalton - I must keep my sense of humour.

We settled down with general chatter about the residents and their needs. Talking with Jan had helped me, and after she left, I had no trouble falling asleep. My last conscious thought centred on how much laundry I had to do.

CHAPTER EIGHTEEN

Dianne

No better place to hear the latest rumours than the *Java Hut*, which is where I parked myself mid-morning. I'd left a message for Sherri but wasn't surprised she hadn't returned my call. Her husband had only been found dead the day before yesterday, after all. And she was bound to have family or close friends who would take priority over my call. Probably not even an obituary yet in the Gazette.

His death was suspicious, and I wondered what the locals would make of it. I went to the counter for a refill and stood in line behind a cluster of teens. Must be nice to have free time from high school classes early in the day.

"Well, my mom's a paramedic and she said the body had been there a while. Gross."

"Cool!"

Had I ever been like that at their age? Like vultures circling for a scrap of carcass, these girls were fixated on all the gory, and imaginative, images the scene provided.

Vulture number one was handed her frothy coffee concoction, along with a stern piece of advice from the server behind the counter. "Mind your opinions, young lady. The poor man may have been somebody's husband, or father. How would you like a member of your family to be discussed in such a way?"

Duly chastised, the girls slunk away to their corner table, but before I could return to my own spot, the giggles had already returned.

Giggle on girls. Life is still ahead of you, and I predict events will bring you maturity. I hope.

Aside from their observations, my morning hadn't produced any results to my satisfaction. I might have more luck at the Tavern, which would open in a few minutes for the lunch crowd.

On my way there I bumped into the Patels and discovered they were headed in the same direction. "Oh, please, Dianne. It would be so nice if you would join us for lunch. Our treat. Isn't that right, babu?"

Bachan nodded. "But of course. We would be most delighted."

Whether he was truly delighted, or polite, I couldn't be sure, but why not?

We settled on a light lunch. They decided to try a local cider and I went with a small glass of wine. They'd walked into town, but I was prepared to offer a ride home.

Bachan remarked on the design of the Tavern. "It is always reminding me of a favourite pub we visited one time in England. The dart board, and beautiful bar. And many fine bottles behind it."

And from there I encouraged them to talk about their travels, which I enjoyed hearing. I haven't done much travelling, so I love to hear where others have been. England was definitely on my bucket list.

I had a question. "I noticed you've placed some beautiful small candles in the front room. Are they for a special occasion?"

Sasitha beamed. "Oh yes, my friend. These are for celebrating Diwali. So important for us."

"Festival of Lights," interjected Bashan. "Lighting these candles, for us, means we are getting rid of the darkness. The darkness can be meaning bad vices, such as greed."

From what I knew of the Patels, greed was a foreign concept to this generous and kind-hearted couple.

"I know about bad vices." I laughed, regretting the comment immediately. "The candles are only temporary, right? I think they give the front room a cozy and welcoming atmosphere for this time of year. And," I looked at Sasitha, "I bet, like most special events, you have specific foods as well?"

Sasitha clapped her hands. "Oh, yes. I am to be teaching Cassie about halwa, pakora and samosa making."

Samosas I quite liked. No doubt some new food items would be cropping up at the dinner table in the next day or two.

As conversations do, it eventually entered a lull. Sasitha had something on her mind, so I helped her out. "Was there something you wanted to ask?"

"Thank you, Dianne. Yes. That is, my husband and I - well, we don't know Alysha as you do, and we are, in our way, so very much concerned for her. Will she be alright?"

The care in her dark brown eyes put me in mind of Jan. These two women were more alike than they realized.

"Alysha will be fine. She is, of course, worried about Jeff's status with the police. As are all of us. But she'll do okay on her own. She's living with all of us, right? How could she not be okay?"

"I told you so, priya. You worry too much." Bachan spoke in a tender voice.

The sweet relationship these two enjoyed made me happy. In the time they'd been with us at Leven Lodge, I'd never heard a sharp word between them. Only kindness and consideration.

And then Sherri Wallis came in. We glanced at each other, and I was about to wave her over, when I noticed she wasn't alone.

Her companion, a middle-aged man, dressed in a suit, and carrying a briefcase, followed her to a corner table.

A lawyer? I wished we were sitting closer.

My focus had shifted from the Patels, and I missed what Sasitha had said. "Sorry, Sasitha. What did you say?"

"I was asking if you could tell me about the theatre. You have discussions with the police, correct? I'm curious to know if you might have heard when the work on it can continue. Bachan and I are so eager to be part of it!"

"I wouldn't exactly say discussions. So, I'm sorry to say I don't have anything new to tell you. Let's hope there will be an update soon. I know Rose is keen to get involved."

"Rose and I, yes, we want to work together with costumes. It will be enjoyable."

"And you, Bachan? I'm thinking you want to see about taking on an acting role, am I right?"

While we talked about the Patels' interest in the new theatre, I managed to keep an eye on Sherri and her companion. Only coffee at their table, so it appeared to be a business meeting. A file folder lay open in front of them. She dabbed at her eyes from time to time and he offered more than one gentle pat on her hand.

"... and so now we must be getting back to our walk. Thank you, Dianne, for sharing this enjoyable time with us." Sasitha had gathered her purse and Bachan had sent our server on his way with payment. By the smile on the young guy's face, he must be enjoying a nice tip as well.

They wanted to stroll, which meant I didn't need to offer to drive, and could hang back for a few minutes to see about a word with Sherri.

"Dianne. You are not now leaving?"

"Um, no, not for a minute, Sasitha. I might have a coffee before I head back. Unless you'd like me to drive you?" Fingers crossed she'd decline.

"We will walk but thank you. Goodbye." Linking arms, they left.

I pulled out my cell phone and made busy with it, while drinking yet another coffee, waiting to see if I could catch Sherri.

My patience was rewarded when her friend left. She remained seated, shoulders slumped, holding her head with one hand.

I moved over toward her table and coughed. "Hi Sherri. Are you okay?"

Her dark hair hung like a curtain around her face, and the wadded tissue in her hand meant I wasn't surprised when she turned a tear-streaked face up to me.

I pulled out a chair and sat. "Hey. What can I do to help?"

"No one can help. No one."

I'll never be accused of being shy about being forward so went for it. "I assume this has to do with your husband? I am so very sorry to hear about him."

"He couldn't have done it. Could he? My lawyer tells me to be wary if the police ask me anything."

Police? Done... what, exactly?

Her sobs had attracted some attention from other tables, and a server appeared to ask if we needed anything. Other than to be left alone, I guessed not. I waved him off.

"How about we get out of here and find somewhere quieter? Or I can take you home if you need a ride?"

She wiped at her face and squeezed her eyes for a moment. Then she took a deep breath and sat up straighter.

"I'm not ready to go home. But I'd be happy to find somewhere to sit for a while."

A couple of benches sat empty near the library in a small park. And bonus, the sun shone overhead. With no breeze, it would be warm enough to sit.

I brushed away a few fallen leaves from the seat. For a moment I enjoyed the sun's rays on my face and didn't comment on the sighs coming from my companion. Best to let her set the pace.

She sniffed. "Do I look like a clown? My nose usually goes bright red and my eyes all puffy when I've been crying." Sherri tried a small smile, which I took as a hopeful sign.

"You should see me when I cry! Blotches and running mascara. Tammy Faye's got nothing on me!"

We shared a laugh, and she relaxed a bit.

"It's so good to be out in the sun." Sherri leaned her head back and closed her eyes.

I thought about her comment that her husband couldn't do it. I debated with myself how to ask, but I needn't have bothered.

"Thanks for coming over to check on me. It's been a rough couple of days. And I'm in limbo with funeral arrangements until the police are done."

"The police? Was he murdered?"

She shook her head. "Might have been easier if he had been. No, not murdered. Suicide."

Oh, damn. Not what I'd expected. "Oh my God, Sherri. I am so sorry. Do you know why?"

"He left a note." She swallowed hard and her eyes filled, but she kept her composure.

When she told me what his note said, I could only speculate what this news would mean to Jeff - and Alysha.

CHAPTER NINETEEN

Alysha

My small-scale office is less than ideal for meeting with multiple visitors. After the receptionist, Christine, ushered Jeff and his new girlfriend into the tight space I felt crowded - and trapped.

"I'm thankful the police released you, Jeff but a phone call would've been fine." Talk about awkward situations. I didn't know what to say in front of *her*. "If they've released you, does that mean the police have a new suspect?"

I didn't offer them a seat, irritated because he'd dragged the vet along. A heads-up would have been nice but then it was Jeff, after all. Understanding emotional complexities within relationships wasn't his strong suit. Gillian hadn't uttered a word. Her narrowed eyes said she preferred to stand back and observe both Jeff and me. Or maybe she felt uncomfortable in here, too. Jeff looked nervous about something and turned to Gillian as if for approval. He cleared his throat before launching into what he'd come to say.

"I, I 'm still a person of interest, according to the police. No explanation. If they have a suspect, or new evidence they're not about to share it with me."

"Makes sense, I guess. Told you not to leave town as well?" I'd say he was stalling, so called him on it. "I'm busy here, so if you have something else to say, let's hear it."

"We were thinking, that is Gillian and I wanted to speak to you in person because we'd like it if we—that is you and I—could still be friends. No hard feelings. I'd still like to take care of the alpacas and..."

Are you kidding me right now? He stopped talking; I assumed as a result of the deliberate glare I shot their way. Standing behind my desk, I leaned forward on both hands, and took my time before speaking. I spoke slowly and hoped my measured tone would convey my sense of betrayal struggling to be heard.

"Listen, I'm not about to act as a woman scorned but I can't pretend I'm not hurt, deeply, by your behaviour. It's much too soon to even talk about being friends. I'll remain considerate with both of you but don't expect an invite for dinner anytime soon." I could feel my blood pressure rising and wanted them out of my office. With a concerted effort, I reduced my indignation level.

I straightened up and moderated my tone. "As for the alpacas, I'm aware of how much they mean to you, but you're not the only one capable of their care, you know, and we will manage. So, once you're settled your living arrangements, I'd prefer it if you didn't come around the barn for the foreseeable future. Who knows if it will change down the road, but it's all I can offer at this time. Now I have a busy day ahead of me so..."

Jeff's shoulders slumped and he was about to respond when Gillian finally spoke. "Leave it, Jeff. Let's go."

To keep my promised civil attitude, I escorted them to the main door, offering grateful thanks no one else worked in the office right now. I wouldn't have unnecessary explaining to do.

Before they reached the door, it flew open and Dianne breezed in. Grand Central Station today. I'd never get any work done if this kept up and half-hoped my face said the same.

"Oops! Sorry." Dianne threw me a look full of questions, but I wouldn't bite. "If you're busy, Alysha, I can come back. Or we can catch up at home later." And then she clued in. "Jeff! You've been released! Terrific - I knew you were innocent. Took the police long enough to come to their senses. Oh, and you must be Gillian?"

I needed to reign this in before she offered to be a bridesmaid at their wedding!

"Dianne, take a seat in my office. Jeff and Gillian are leaving."

Her eyes were wide to match the excitement in her voice. "But what I wanted to tell you would be of interest to Jeff and...Gillian. About the murder."

Damn! Her comment stopped the couple dead in their tracks. I tried to keep control. "You know I don't want to hear gossip, Dianne. Why don't you leave it to the police?"

"I know, I know. They probably know most of this already." She looked at Jeff. "But I thought it might put Jeff's mind at ease if he heard it from someone other than the cops."

Hearing the remark, Gillian grabbed Jeff's elbow. I began to see who called the shots in their relationship. "We should hear what she has to say." And then she tossed the grenade. "I'm sure you'd like to know whatever affects Jeff as well, wouldn't you, Alysha?"

I gave up. Outnumbered, I led them to a small meeting room. Marginally bigger than my office, but at least it had chairs for all.

I back-pedalled, keeping my thoughts to myself while Jeff pulled up a chair close to Gillian. Dianne, at least, had the grace to look as if she realised she'd stepped in it.

Inwardly I fumed. "Goodness, where are my manners? I'll order us coffee and cake while we play happy families, shall I?" Sarcasm may be Dianne's forte, and I rarely indulge, but this occasion called for it. By the smile tugging at her mouth, I must have pulled it off.

I'd savour the small victory later. "Okay, Dianne, what's so important?" Jeff and Gillian leaned in eagerly to listen. "I have an appointment in a few minutes, so let's speed things up."

Dianne managed to appear contrite, if only for a moment. Reluctantly, I found myself pulled into hearing about the conversation she'd had with Sherri Wallis. Most of it I'd heard before, but Dianne elaborated on the discovery of Brock Wallis's body for Jeff's benefit. The suicide note was new information, and I found myself curious to learn what it contained.

"What did the note say, Dianne?" asked Jeff.

Gillian laid a hand on his arm to quell his enthusiasm. "Don't interrupt. She'll tell us."

Dianne slowed her speech down, as if to bring a semblance of respect to what she had to say. "I don't like to speak ill of the dead but according to Sherri, her husband, Brock, was a heavy drinker and a gambler. He'd managed his debts until recently. At least up until April Lancashire had questioned discrepancies in the invoices he prepared for work on the theatre."

Jeff jumped to his feet. "He killed her because of that! He didn't want to be found out! I'd heard them arguing but I liked the guy. Everybody liked him. But murder!"

Dianne held up a hand. "Jeff, sit down. Let me finish first." Jeff sat. His eyes bright and shining after his outburst. "Sorry. Go on."

When she had our attention, she continued. "So, the note. According to Sherri, her husband feared he might have killed her - during a drink-related blackout. His angst over possibly killing her, combined with his disgrace at having his money problems discovered was too much." Dianne frowned and continued with a voice full of sadness. "In the note, he said he loved her, but she'd be better off if he was gone. He hoped she would forgive him."

I don't think I'd been prepared for that revelation. I felt shocked that Sherri, who barely knew Dianne, would have shared so much pain with her. But who was I to judge? "Dianne. Did Sherri say these blackouts were a regular thing?"

She nodded. "Yes, apparently it happened when he drank too much."

Gillian coughed and spoke up, confident in her relationship with Jeff. "While I'm not unsympathetic to what you've told us, Dianne, what makes you think his suicide confession confirms he is the murderer? If the man had no real recollection of the deed how does that help Jeff?"

Yes, she liked to be in charge. So did I! "Whoa. Hold on, Gillian. It was Jeff who jumped to the assumption. Dianne, I believe, is only re-telling what she has been told." Something about Jeff's new love interest rubbed me the wrong way and I relished coming to Dianne's defence. "If the police weren't considering his suicide as an indication of guilt, why would they release Jeff?"

Jeff's head had snapped back and forth trying to keep up. "Alysha's right, Gillian. Otherwise, why would they let me go. Free of any charges?"

Gillian's pursed lips suggested she and Jeff might be having a discussion of sorts, once away from here. I tried not to gloat.

Dianne added her usual two cents. "Let's not underestimate our police force. I'm confident they're on the track of the killer."

Jeff nodded and I recognized the desperate look he had on his face; wishing he were somewhere else. Probably with the alpacas. Good luck on that score.

I needed to focus on my job. Jeff and Gillian had taken enough of my time. I summarised, "So, let's leave it that Jeff has been cleared. None of us knew Brock, so we're in no position to comment on guilt or innocence. Leave it to the authorities - that's why we pay taxes." I stood and opened the door. "Time to call it a day."

Dianne was the first to leave. "I'll see you at home, Alysha."

Jeff and Gillian made a move to follow. Jeff hesitated and turned to me. "Thanks for seeing us and hearing us out. I'll respect your wishes about me coming around, but would you mind if I took one last walk around the barn to say goodbye to the alpacas? It would mean a great deal to me."

Oh geez, he would pull that one on me. "No, no, go ahead." I stood straighter and spoke to them both. "I wish you both the best of luck. Goodbye." Because, Jeff, you're going to need luck with Gillian!

I watched them leave, then went to my office, where I shut the door and collapsed in my chair. It's really over. My relationship with Jeff is done!

Had Brock Wallis killed April Lancashire. And if not, who?

CHAPTER TWENTY

Dianne

After I left Alysha's office, my excitement at being able to share what I'd learned from Sherri Wallis had been dampened by the uncomfortable tension I'd barged into. Her break-up with Jeff saddened me more than I might want to admit. She appeared to be handling it well, and her new career would be a healthy distraction. I'd have to see what Jan and I could do to help her through.

I decided to stop at *Sweet Things* for an addition to whatever meal we'd be having later. A few minutes later a box of freshly made tarts sat in the back of my car. Lemon, custard, and blueberry – enough variety for all. And of course, butter tarts!

I had almost reached home when I stopped the car and rolled down the window. "Hi Cory. Need a lift?"

My young protégé seemed eager to accept the ride. "Sure, thanks!" He hopped in.

"Your backpack must weigh a ton! Lots of homework?"

"Not exactly. I picked up some books at the library. Have you ever heard of James Herriot? He was a vet in England, mostly farm animals, years and years ago. I've got a book about a lot of his experiences." He shrugged his shoulders. "I thought it might give me some idea of how vets worked before things were modern."

"Oh, you mean like having electricity and cars?"

He laughed. "It's not that old!"

"Sounds like a splendid book. There's also been a TV series you might want to watch. I've seen it – *years and years ago*!" We both laughed. "So, are you enjoying working at Leven Lodge?"

He gave me two-thumbs up as his answer.

I debated whether I should mention anything about Jeff no longer being there. What the heck. "I guess you know Jeff won't be around the place now. You may end up with more responsibility. Frank's not as young as he used to be, and Philip... Well, Philip is not exactly full-time, if you get my drift."

He shifted a bit on the seat next to me. Had my comment about Jeff made him uncomfortable? "Yes, I knew about Jeff, he's really expert about the alpacas. And Philip? I kinda like him. He's smart, you know. He asked me a lot of questions when he learned I'd like to be a vet."

We pulled up to the house. "I'm glad you're here, Cory. And for the record, I'm proud of how you're doing in school and that you have goals."

He didn't respond, but the flush in his cheeks said my remarks meant something. "Off you go now. Don't forget to grab your snack in the kitchen."

I watched him sprint down the side of the house. He'd never walk through the front door, but always came in through the kitchen. Jan had become fond of him as well, and on the days he helped out, she found time to put together an after-school snack that was more like a full course meal.

My thoughts went back to Alysha. I hadn't truly considered what Jeff's absence might mean regarding the alpacas and other chores. We didn't exactly have anyone here full-time time for their care. Alysha might have to reconsider whether banning Jeff was a wise economical idea, at least until finding someone else to help. I didn't see Bachan filling the role!

I headed inside. No happy hour scheduled today, but Nina had parked herself in the media room, channel surfing. "No Bennett time today?" I teased her as I came into the room. My voice roused a sleepy Hemingway, curled up in her lap. He sniffed, then dismissed me as insignificant and went back to sleep.

"Hi, chickie. No, he's got some old boys club meeting or something tonight. I'm killing time till after dinner. Then I'm into some re-writes on the twins' memoir."

She seemed eager to talk, so I discarded my jacket and sank into a recliner, putting the box of tarts on the nearest table. "And how's that coming along?"

She shut off the TV. "You know, I'm convinced I'm going to be able to build an engaging story about family dynamics around their childhood. Fictional of course but based on much of what they've been telling me." She lowered her voice and leaned in. "Poor Lily always gets the short end of the stick. Been that way for years, and I'm beginning to see a pattern."

"Families. Can't pick them, can you?"

She laughed. "So true. Now what have you been doing today?"

I filled her in, and the talk of April Lancashire's murder cast a pall in the room. I tried to get us back to a lighter vein. "At least Jeff's no longer under suspicion. The police must imagine Brock is a solid suspect. But how does a dead person defend themself?"

"You never said how he died?"

I thought of the anguish on Sherri's face as she revealed her husband had hanged himself. I wouldn't wish that on anyone. Nina didn't comment when I said I preferred not to say, out of respect for the family.

"No matter. I'll have to make some notes on this case for future reference."

Nina, the opportunist. Well, she'd changed her mind about using Leven Lodge as basis for a murder story, we'd see how she got on with April Lancashire's case. "Make sure if you write about it, it's an original story."

"Oh, my God! I completely forgot!" Nina's exclamation caused Hemingway to jump from her lap and scuttle to the other side of the couch. I didn't know dogs could look offended.

"What?"

"About an original idea. I should talk to the police!"

Then I remembered. "Oh, you mean the plagiarising thing?"

"You know about it?"

"Something I heard from Cassie's want-to-be suitor. That Griffith Sharples. He said he'd overheard an argument." I raised an eyebrow at Nina. "How did *you* hear about it?"

"Dianne, Dianne. You've lived in this small town longer than I have. Do I really need to explain?"

Grant's Crossing still has a mill – the rumour kind!

"Right. Well, when I heard pretty-boy Sharples talk about it, I suggested he tell the police. I'd forgotten until you reminded me. Just before we found out Jeff had been arrested. I wonder if he ever did tell the police?"

"Well, sunshine. I aim to find out." She opened a small notebook and flipped through some pages. "There. I knew I wrote it down. See if this jives with what you heard. Kyle Foreman writes plays. Has written several over the years, with some minor success. He claims somebody named Matthew Fielding stole his latest written play and sold it to Countryside as his own piece of work. Apparently visibly upset with April Lancashire when he learned she'd been the one to buy it. Wanted recognition – or retribution."

"Retribution. Meaning murder? Yes, Nina - we need to make sure the police hear about this!"

I had my cell phone out in the blink of an eye. "I'd like to speak to someone in charge of the April Lancashire case."

Nina's appetite for a story source had her hanging on my every word. She deflated a bit when I told her I was on hold. And then I heard the voice of DC Dubois. I identified myself and asked him if he'd heard about the rumours around town regarding a significant row April had engaged in over a potentially plagiarised play.

"Ms. Mitchell. We appreciate this information and will pursue this as the investigation warrants. Thank you for calling."

Wow. I've been brushed off before, but the speed of his dismissal set a new record.

"Chickie, I'd say they already know. He didn't ask for name spellings, or other details. But you know how they like to 'no comment'. Sounds like it to me."

Cassie poked her head into the room. "Dinner in about twenty minutes."

Oh, right. Dinner. I pointed to the box. "In there Cassie, something extra for dessert."

Her face lit up. "Sweet! I only had ice-cream planned, so thanks!" She grabbed the box and headed back to the kitchen.

I stood. "I need to clean up before dinner, see you in a little bit."

She gathered up her stuff and clipped the lead onto Hemingway's collar. "Snuggums needs a walkie before then, too."

"Oh, and Nina. I don't know if Alysha will be joining us for dinner, but I think we need to let her set pace for conversation, and don't let on I told you about what happened in her office, okay?" I surprised myself, worried I'd be accused of spreading rumours. Guess Alysha's influence has affected me.

"I agree. The poor girl doesn't need it dragged out. Maybe she needs a night out to let loose for a few hours."

Not a bad idea. Although the last time Alysha, Nina and I had gone out, it didn't go quite as planned.

We had moved out into the hallway, with Nina headed toward the front door, and me to the stairs,

Hemingway let out an excited yelp as the door opened and Alysha entered. She looked a lot better than when I'd last seen her. Energised, almost. "Ladies. Exactly who I wanted to see. I've been thinking we need a girls' night out. What do you say?"

Nina and I burst out laughing.

CHAPTER TWENTY-ONE

Alysha

I'd asked Jan to join us for our girls' night out but she'd other plans. She enjoyed swimming at the nearby *Y* twice a week, and this was one of her nights. I'm sure we could manage to cause enough trouble on our own.

Nina had the foresight to order Uber to take us to the only Italian restaurant in town. *The Olive House* was a new venue, but I'd heard good things about their menu and was eager to sample. Lately the Patel's curry preferences have dominated our repertoire at the Lodge, and I had a craving for pasta!

The Chianti flowed and loosened tongues. Dianne knows I'm not fond of hearsay, so she kept the conversation neutral, at least to start. We discussed the progress of Nina's memoir on the twins and dissected what she'd learned about their relationship. According to Nina it was sure to be a bestseller! That might be, but if what Nina now revealed about their childhood proved true, I'd start to see Lily in a new light.

Then Dianne had a turn when the subject focused on her involvement with Cory. To my surprise, she'd taken the maternal role in her stride, and it suited her. He seemed mutually fond of her too, so it's a good match for them both.

Not to be left out, I knew they wanted details of my failed relationship with Jeff and how I'd handle running the Lodge on my own. No surprise Nina was overly interested! She's a woman always on the hunt for a story angle. I was sober enough to answer her. "Nina, I don't *need* a man to run Leven Lodge." I sipped my wine, which provided a little more courage and continued. "You of all people should know a woman is not defined by, or has need of, a man to help her run her life." Then I concentrated on the tantalising lasagne that had just been served.

I expected a retort from Nina, but none came. Instead, Dianne who broke the silence with a laugh. "Right, girlfriend. Tell us how you really feel. You know both Nina and I only have your best interest at heart, right?"

I swallowed a mouthful of delectable noodles and sauce, before I replied. "I know you're concerned but put your mind at rest. If I need help with the alpacas, or anything else at the Lodge, I'll hire someone. I might love the creatures, but you won't see me mucking out the barn. I'm sure once Cory learns the ropes from Frank and Philip they will manage. We just have to give them a chance."

I changed the subject. "Now then, Nina, you managed to drag yourself away from Bennett's clutches this evening. I'm glad he gave you the night off. You'll give me loads of warning if I need to rent out your room, won't you?"

Nina looked coy and smiled at me. "You'll be the first to know, sunshine."

Dianne chuckled and appeared to be enjoying the change of pace from the usual dinner talk with other folks back at the lodge. "What's so funny Dianne or do we need to cut off your supply of wine?"

Dianne put her empty wine glass down. "No, it's not the wine. I was laughing at how adept you are at changing the conversation away from yourself. You're not getting off that easy until you tell us how you feel about Jeff and his...conquest. Or was it the other way round?"

I considered what they both wanted to know for all of thirty seconds. They wouldn't get any details, or observations of Jeff's relationship dynamics, from me. "I know nothing of the ins and outs of Jeff and Gillian's romance. And I don't want to! These things happen. It's over and we're going our separate ways. So... I've asked Jeff to get on with the next chapter in his life and he's moved out of the lodge. End of story, and I wish them both well."

Dianne frowned. "I'll miss him, but it was meant to be, I guess." She did look sad. I know she's fond of Jeff, but that's life. We all need to move on.

We finally hit on other topics. Halloween was coming and Nina was on it like glue on a stamp, with ideas for decoration themes, and asking how many kids we might expect. I let her and Dianne have at it. I'm not a big fan of Halloween. Last year, Jeff and I had taken off for the evening, preferring to be away from the trick or treaters. Then our table talk briefly touched on the murder investigation, but Dianne seemed reluctant to discuss anything to do with the Wallis' and I let it be. Although I was a little surprised, she dismissed the opportunity to embellish on what she knew. I waited for the other shoe to drop.

Dessert, and then coffee soon followed. We had eaten well, and I was glad I'd suggested we have an evening out. It might have been just what I needed.

As we lingered over our coffee I thought about our conversation. Yes, I'll miss him too but then I thought about the future and smiled. The sky's the limit.

***

Next morning saw me swearing off red wine as I swallowed a couple of painkillers for my throbbing headache. I sat in my office mulling over property listings I'd selected to show my next client, due at ten o'clock. He was late but it gave my headache time to disappear. Maybe I should cut back on the coffee as well as the red wine. I'd been jumpy all morning and had become so engrossed in paperwork that when Christine knocked on my door I started. She ushered in my new client - Kyle Foreman. I prayed he had a quiet voice to go with his dressed-down attire. Business casual well suited to a tanned and relaxed face.

"How do you do, Mr. Foreman. Please take a seat."

He shook my hand. "I apologise for being late. And please, call me Kyle."

"And I'm Alysha. Thanks for coming to see me. I'm looking forward to helping you find the perfect property. You did say when you called you were trying to find an investment property but let's be more specific. For starters, is this a single-family home or a commercial structure you're interested in?"

His prolonged silence, as he scrutinized me, made me uncomfortable. And then out came the dreaded comment. "So, Alysha, have you been doing this long? You don't look old enough to have a driver's licence, never mind a real estate licence."

I should be used to people taking me for younger than my almost thirty years. Once again, I needed more than a business suit and heels. I could have screamed a protest, but..., oh, who cares besides me anyway?

"Let me assure you... Kyle, I'm fully qualified. I'll be branching out before long and plan to have my own brokerage soon."

Kyle's face broke out in a grin. "My apologies, I've a daughter about your age and I can't imagine her in your position. She's at home looking after her two young boys. My grandchildren."

I relaxed my guard and berated myself for making quick assumptions. I should probably work on my people skills. "Kyle, don't take this personally, but you're living in the dark ages. Being a parent is hard work and I would imagine it's training for anything she wants to do in the future. As for me, I also have experience in running a home. A retirement home. I'm the owner and operator of Leven Lodge, so, as you can see, looks can be deceiving."

"I don't take it personally at all. Someone needs to set me straight." Recognition flashed across his face. "Wait. Your name is Grant? Grant's Crossing - is there a connection? My family and I have lived here for years and are well acquainted with the Grant name. Related?"

Pride washed over me. "Yes, you're right. My ancestors founded Grant's Crossing in the 1800's. So, I know more than a little about this area. Now let's get down to business. Unless you prefer someone...older to assist you?"

He held up his hands and laughed in a good-natured way. "That won't be necessary Alysha. I have utmost confidence in you."

***

After hashing out a few details we left the office to assess his current home for current market value. Kyle and his wife were looking to downsize to a smaller home, but they were also in the market for an investment property where they could derive some income. I couldn't help but be challenged, and excited, at the prospect of a multi-property transaction.

Once the appraisal of his comfortable and modern home had been completed, we agreed to stop for lunch before viewing some of the listings I'd put together. We continued our discussion at the *Java Hut*. After-effects of the red wine lingered, and the best I could handle was a bowl of soup.

Bennett, as my mentor, had instilled in me a mantra; *Get to know what makes your client tick to help you pin down what they like. But don't get too friendly*. When we'd settled in a booth, I asked a personal question.

"And what do you do for a living, Kyle, or are you retired?"

He burst out laughing. "Shoe's on the other foot now. I think you made the same assumption as I did with you. I supposed you looked too young for the job, and you assumed I was ready for the one-foot-in-the-grave-brigade because I have white hair."

I joined him in the laughter. "Touché. You got me there. You don't have to answer . but I do like to get to know my clients."

"Ask away. I'm only joking with you."

Over our coffee I learned of his long career as a playwright. He'd been modestly successful over the years and was excited to offer his latest play to April Lancashire for her approval. Having a local theatre in Grant's Crossing where he lived appealed to him.

Talk of the theatre led to talk of the murder. I asked when he'd last seen the victim. His face clouded over, and he began to shred the paper napkin in front of him. I wasn't sure what had upset him and waited to see if he'd explain.

"We met a couple of days before the murder. She knew I was coming to see her with a new play I'd written, and I thought it would be perfect for the debut of the new venue." He jutted his jaw and tightened his lips. "Imagine my surprise to learn she had considered another play - with a similar storyline. My play, *Jamieson Strikes Out*, is about minor league baseball and how its main character deals with being offered a major league contract. Sorry, I digress. When I noticed the similarities, I asked to see a copy. She handed me *Minor Strikeout*, written by Matthew Fielding. As I skimmed the first few pages, I realised it was my play!"

"How can that be? How did he get your play to use as his own?"

"He bloody plagiarized it! Then I learned April had accepted it, before even seeing mine, which she'd promised they would use. To say I was livid is an understatement."

Was it just me, or had I stumbled across another murder suspect? Did Dubois know about this? My wandering thoughts were stopped when Kyle continued.

"I'm sorry, Alysha. I didn't mean to get upset. As you might guess, this has soured me on the industry. If this doesn't get resolved to my satisfaction, I may turn my back on a career I love. Which is why my wife and I need to consider other forms of income. Hence an investment property."

"Kyle, it would be a real shame if you were to give up something you love. Why don't take a little time before making a decision?"

"You may be right, but in the meantime, I need to have options."

"Of course. I'm quite sure I can find an investment property that will work well. Perhaps as a short-term rental. You know, with the new spa and now the theatre, there will be an influx of tourists who might want a temporary place to stay."

He brightened. "Excellent idea."

I made some notes, but my mind wanted to get back to the confrontation between him and April Lancashire over his work. "How did April take the news when you told her the play was originally your own work? And another question - if you don't know Matthew Fielding, how did he get a copy of your work?"

Kyle's face turned grey, and he took his time before answering. "Even after I confronted April about my lost revenue and more importantly my credibility, she wasn't too concerned when I accused her of not vetting the people who contribute to the theatre. As for how Fielding managed to steal my work... Well, I've been trying to sell it for a while, so I'd sent it far and wide hoping for a buyer. All online of course, so it's been known to happen. There are unscrupulous people everywhere."

Oh, how well I knew that to be a fact!

The lunchtime crowd had thinned and only a few customers lingered. I glanced up and noticed a police car outside. Dubois and his partner strode into the cafe looking around. I thought maybe for a coffee break, until they headed in our direction. Dubois wore his official face.

"Afternoon Ms. Grant. Sorry to interrupt but I'd like a word with Mr. Foreman."

"This must be official, Detective. Using my last name again?"

"Correct." He looked at Kyle who hadn't spoken but frowned in a puzzled way.

"Mr. Foreman. Would you mind coming to the police station with us? We've a few questions you might be able to help us with concerning the murder of April Lancashire."

Talk about timing! I looked at Kyle. I didn't know him well enough to decipher the expression on his face. Had he been waiting for the police to contact him, or was he taken by surprise? He pushed away from the table and stood.

"Right, detective. I planned to see you anyway. I want Mathew Fielding charged with plagiarism of my latest play."

Dubois and Truman glanced at each other and then escorted Kyle Foreman out of the cafe. Kyle turned as he reached the door and gave me a thumbs up.

Does he know how much trouble he could be in?

CHAPTER TWENTY-TWO

Dianne

"I'm sorry you missed out on the evening, Jan. We had a fun time, and I think it benefitted Alysha to have a night out." I chuckled. "She might not be enjoying the results this morning though."

I'd hung back after breakfast to catch up with our housekeeper. Like me, she had concern for Alysha, but after last night I felt our girl would be fine. Time to move forward. It might be more interesting to focus on the relationship growing in leaps and bounds between Nina and Bennett, which had moved at a breakneck pace. Alysha's comment for Nina to let her know about renting out her room hit the mark, I think. Nina can be verbose most of the time, but when it comes to Bennett, she's playing it close to the chest.

Jan smiled. "Yes, I saw Alysha for a quick minute when she left for work. She did mention a headache." She gave one last swipe at the counter and put her dishcloth down. "Truthfully, I'm more worried about Cassie right now."

Oh yay, something else to talk about. "Oh, yes? And where is our pot-smoking gossip?" I asked as I looked down the hall.

"Not here; I sent her into town for supplies. It's that Griffith Sharples fellow. She's now confided in me she doesn't know how to deal with him. He won't take no for an answer and from what I can tell, he's bordering on an obsession over her."

I had to agree with her. "I've seen the way he is around her as well. Has that kind of pathetic lost puppy way about him. I don't think she's ever encouraged him, other than to meet for an occasional coffee. He obviously wants more from her than she's willing to offer."

Jan's brow knitted. "I feel I'm a reasonable judge of character, but I can't get a read on him. He's polite and has an innocent kind of charm.

He appears to be well read and intelligent. But can't hold a job and doesn't take well to disappointment when Cassie tries to rebuff him."

"Well, we're good at supporting each other around here, so if she needs help, she knows to call on us. And I'd bet her dad will be watching as well. At the end of the day, I'd size up Griffith as too passive for her taste. In her words he's a nice, bland, guy. Not a ringing endorsement, is it?"

Jan laughed. "No, I don't see Cassie settling for his type. But she may need to be more assertive in setting boundaries with him."

"Boundaries? Who needs boundaries – it's not my darling precious again is it? Has he been digging where he's not supposed to?" Nina had swept into the kitchen, with her usual knack of interrupting a conversation.

Jan's lips tightened at the mention of Hemingway. She would never be fond of the ankle-biter. "Did you want coffee, Nina?" She eyed the empty mug in Nina's hand.

"Coffee? Oh, yes. I was hoping there'd be a fresh pot on?"

Jan took the mug from her hand to fill with fresh brew. While Jan busied herself, I answered Nina. "The boundaries we were talking about refer to Cassie's would-be boyfriend. She's not interested in him, but he's persistent."

"Oh, him. Yes, I've noticed a distinct lack of fireworks between them. She should send him packing if he's not her type. Thanks, Jan." She gave us a theatrical sniff of the hot drink as Jan handed over the mug. "Answer me this. Why does coffee never taste as good as it smells? Right, I don't know either. Okay, then I'll leave you both to your discussion. Back to the computer for me. Oh, and Jan, I'll be staying at Bennett's tonight, so won't be here for dinner."

"Why don't you just move in with him, for goodness's sake. You spend more time there than here. I don't see how you ever get much writing done!" Jan's sharp tone took me aback.

If I were to guess, I'd say Nina had worn out her welcome with Jan. Or maybe it was Hemingway that had overstayed.

"Now then, Jan. A lady shouldn't be rushed into something they're not ready for. That's what you'd say to Cassie wouldn't you?" Nina's condescending tone wouldn't go over well with Jan.

"Oh! I have work to do and can't be nattering over nothing all day. Excuse me." Jan didn't often get flustered, but Nina always hit the mark. And to be fair I don't think it's intentional. Those two are like oil and water, or nitro-glycerine and dynamite. Jan wouldn't be sorry if Nina pulled up stakes and moved on. The sooner the better.

So, my time with Jan ended and Nina headed back up to her writing lair. I decided to head into town and see what I could pick up for Halloween treats.

***

I still managed to avoid the grocery store and found a bountiful selection of sugary treats at the *Barrel Barn*. Years ago, so I've been told, Grant's Crossing had a distillery and when it folded the location was bought and developed by a food merchant, who saw potential in the abandoned barrels and distillery décor. One corner was devoted to party supplies, and they could be counted on for terrific seasonal selections.

Opening the door, I savoured the aromas of various spices. I'd never been a cook, but this place could be inspirational. Not sure of exactly what I'd be buying, I opted for a small cart to push instead of carrying a basket. I soon had it filled with paper black cats and witch's hats. A variety of bagged candy nestled inside an inflatable pumpkin.

"You've been busy, I see." Alysha's elbow bumped mine. Her face didn't reflect the light-hearted greeting she offered me but sported a frown of consternation. I noticed she held a basket with assorted candies and a few orange and black items.

"What's with this? You don't like Halloween."

"Not for me. I was *voluntold* to pick a variety of things up for the office. Seems my boss is a big kid at heart. He has one of the largest plastic cauldrons I've ever seen and wants it filled to the brim with candy." She looked down at her purchases. "Maybe I should throw in some toothbrushes as well."

"And deprive local dentists of revenue. For shame, Ms. Grant!"

She laughed and the frown faded. "Are you doing any other shopping, or heading back home?"

"Hadn't planned to do anything else. Is there something I can do for you?"

Alysha shook her head. "No, thanks. Unless you have time to grab a coffee with me? I'd like to tell you a bit about my day – and away from the lodge."

'Got it.' Curiosity goes better with coffee. We paid for our purchases and ambled over to the *Java Hut*. Late afternoon meant it wasn't busy and the high school kids had come and gone.

We settled at a window-side table and pushed open the lids on our coffee cups. "So, what's up. Something happen at the office?"

Seeing as Alysha disliked spreading gossip, I didn't expect a whole lot of speculation. Dry facts would likely be the order of the day.

"Sort of." Alysha took another sip. "I have myself a new client, or at least I hope he'll be a client, if he's not arrested."

She has a way of dropping bombs like it's no big deal. "Arrested? Who, what...c'mon spill it!"

I bet she did it deliberately just to see my reaction. Another accomplished button-pusher it would seem. Or maybe I've made my buttons too easy to target.

Alysha told me about her new client, the plagiarism angle and how Dubois and Truman came to take him to the station with them for a little chat.

I sat back and held up my hand and counted. "So, we have Kyle Foreman, and Brock Wallis as definite suspects in the murder." I held up two fingers. "Jeff is a no brainer and doesn't count."

"Makes you wonder who else will crawl out of the woodwork. I'd say the police have their hands full on this case. I hate to jump to conclusions—especially when the person can't defend themselves—but I'd say Brock Wallis is the number one suspect." Alysha sipped at her coffee before continuing. "Have you spoken with his wife lately? How's she doing?"

Perfect. She'd found another button and I downplayed the tremor of guilt pricking at my conscience. "On my list to do later today. I don't want to pester her, you know? Ironically the first time we had coffee in here, I thought there might be hope of a friendship. I'm trying to find the balance."

Without forethought, I tapped one of Alysha's buttons. "Too bad Dax isn't still around. We'd have more chance of knowing what's going on."

She flushed a little but didn't take the bait. "I'm sure the officers in charge will let us know any time there's something directly affecting us."

"You're probably right. I should be grateful it's not me under the magnifying glass this time."

"Oh, Dianne. It's not always about you!"

Whoa! I raised an eyebrow at her and she backed down. "I'm sorry. That was uncalled for. For what it's worth I hope you and Sherri do strike up a friendship after this is resolved. She could probably use a good friend. And I know you have it in you."

I teased. "To be a good friend?"

"Yes. Both you and Jan have been supportive of me since day one, so there!"

The air had cleared, and we finished our coffee. "What happens now with your new client?"

Alysha frowned. "He verbally agreed to let me do the listing for his home, but nothing's official. I'll have to wait to hear back from him. Although, I'll be optimistic and get back to the office and finish drawing up the paperwork.'

"Unless he's the murderer?"

"Please don't make jokes, Dianne. I, for one, am sick of hearing about it. It's managed to reach into every aspect of my life. Personal and work."

"Sorry, kiddo. You're right. Now that Jeff's cleared, let's try not to talk about it. Life goes on. I'd better let you get back to work, or should I say office decorating. And I need to get my Halloween stash back to the lodge. Will you be with us for dinner tonight?"

She smiled. "Yep, I'd planned to be there, but just in case, can you let Jan know when you go back? And now I need to go. Thanks for the coffee. See you later."

***

We went our separate ways and I arrived back at Leven Lodge. No surprise to see Nina's car missing; parked in Bennett's driveway I'd say. I ran up to my room, saying hi to a few of the residents on the way. I didn't stop for chit chat and needed to call Sherri while my resolve stayed strong.

"Hi Dianne. I'm glad you called. I've had a hell of a day. Any chance you'd like to come by this evening. The place is a mess, but I'll explain. I have wine?"

"If you're up for company, I'll drop over. Um, I just need your address."

She gave me detailed instructions because, no surprise, the Wallis home was out in the country. "You'll see *Brodan Construction* on the mailbox."

"I can be there at about seven?"

"See you then."

I hung-up and then decided on a quick shower before dinner, briefly considering the possibility of whether it would be curry, or a Cassie creation.

***

To my happy surprise, we had barbecued hamburgers, and salads for dinner. "One last time for the grill before the weather changes," explained Jan.

Juicy tomatoes, sweet red onions, and various condiments were enjoyed by all. Followed by pie. Contented faces all around. Conversation had been light. Suggestions for Halloween took up most of the talk.

"You're in a rush, Dianne?" Alysha didn't miss much.

"Sorry, yes. I'm off to see Sherri and should be making tracks."

"Ah. Good for you. Hope she's okay."

I pushed away from the table, hoping to avoid questions. Ears had pricked up at the mention of her name. "Me, too. Night all."

I scooted up to my room to grab my keys and a jacket and then headed out. I loved this time of year but didn't care for the nights growing dark so early. Not a star in the sky, so I was glad of Sherri's directions. Finding a country home in the dark can be a challenge.

I'd never have seen the home from the road. The mailbox was the only clue. A thick wall of evergreen trees on either side of a lengthy paved driveway gave way to an open space and as I pulled my car nearer the front entrance, I couldn't help but stare.

What an impressive home! Quarried block-stone, grey and white trim. Two full stories with dormer windows over a triple car garage. About a hundred feet away from the house stood a darkened work shed – the official Brodan office. Two pickup trucks were parked nearby. I wondered how Brock's death would affect the business they had built. And then hoped I'd be up to the task of offering comfort and support if it were required.

I took a deep breath and stepped up to the double-wide front entrance and knocked.

Sherri answered. She didn't look any better than when I'd last seen her and offered a tired smile. "Come on in." She stood back and I entered a spacious foyer, marble floor...and a mess. Cushions on the floor, crooked wall hangings, drawer contents tossed over the floor.

I shook my head in disbelief. "What the hell?"

With a resigned shoulder shrug, she explained. "Cops had a search warrant. They left a few hours ago, but I can't get motivated to start cleaning up."

I scrambled for words of comfort. Hallmark doesn't make a greeting card for this occasion, so I settled for my typical fall-back. "Let's get you a drink and sit. Where do you keep the good stuff? I think we need something a little stronger than wine, am I right?"

She summoned another weak smile and pointed toward a cabinet, whose doors hung open. Good stuff was right. Bottles in that collection were beyond my budget. I recognized a respectable name and pulled out a bottle of brandy. One glass had been broken—did they have to be that careless! —but I found a couple undamaged and poured us a decent medicinal dose.

"Geeze. How much searching did they do?" I pushed her ahead of me into a magazine-approved living room, and straightened cushions on a large sectional sofa. We sat and I waited.

"I thought it excessive, but they're looking for anything to back up the discrepancies in billing to give credence to why Brock... To why he's dead. From ledger books to flash drives. Guess they figured if something was worth hiding it might not be in the office space. The one officer did apologize after he knocked over the glasses, but whatever."

"Drink up," I urged. She sipped, as did I. I appreciated the warmth of the mellow liquid as it trickled down my throat and I hoped it would bring some calm to the shell-shocked woman next to me.

"He couldn't have killed her. I won't believe it for a second that he did. I don't know what I'll do without him." Then the sobs started. I supplied tissue and let the tears run their course. She must have been emotionally spent because it didn't last long. She tossed back the rest of her brandy and refilled the glass.

"They never show you the mess on television of the aftermath when a place is searched, do they?" She let her gaze drift around the room, shaking her head. "We built this home fifteen years ago. And when I say *we* built, I mean it. Hands on. Both of us. I might be the paper pusher now, but in the beginning we worked together. I can frame and drywall as well as anyone. Every inch of this home has our mark on it. And now, I don't know if I want to be here without Brock."

She was hurting. Not bad enough her husband was gone, but that his death could be a sign of guilt in the murder. I couldn't imagine. "Sherri, I truly don't know what to say. This is beyond horrible. You've lost your husband and your home is torn apart." Before I knew it the words tumbled out. "What can I do to help? I'm here now and I don't mind getting my hands dirty and start putting this place back together."

She took another healthy swallow and nodded at me. "You're very kind, Dianne. Especially considering we haven't known each other long. For now, I'm glad of some company. I'll be on the phone tomorrow. Some of my guys will come and help me tidy things up. What I really need at this moment is someone to talk to."

Well, okay then. I began to wonder about her friends. She must have friends, and family? "Whatever I can do to help. Did the police say anything? Take anything?"

"I couldn't bear to see them go through the office things out back, so I stayed here, but watched from the window. I heard them mention tax evasion and gambling debts. Boxes and boxes of stuff were taken. Plus, his laptop. And no, they worked tight-lipped. It's as if the ground beneath my feet is no longer solid, you know? That I can't count on anything anymore. Except myself."

"I have some news that might help." I proceeded to tell her what I'd learned from Alysha regarding Kyle Foreman. "So, there might be at least one other suspect." I tried to sound encouraging but the words sounded flat to my ears.

"You know, April Lancashire wasn't an easy person to work with. You could talk to my work crew—which I told the police to do—and they'd tell you stories of how rude and demanding she could be. I don't know why the Countryside Players put up with her for as long as they did."

I leaned over and patted the top of her leg. "The police have a lot of suspects to weed through. Try not to worry too much. Even though your husband's death points a lot of suspicion his way, it seems circumstantial."

"I hope you're right, Dianne. Thirty-five years, and now I have to ask myself how well I knew him at all."

When I left a couple of hours later, she'd fallen asleep on the sofa. I found a blanket to cover her, and quietly let myself out. Before I could turn the ignition in my car, my phone buzzed. It was Alysha.

"If you're done at Sherri's we could use your help over here. I'm not sure whether to call the police or not, but Griffith Sharples is here and won't leave!"

CHAPTER TWENTY-THREE

Alysha

I'd called Dianne hoping she'd help us with this Griffith Sharples situation. I'm no stranger to drunks and their behaviour from my university years but nothing like this. He was starting to scare me. Alcohol had the ability to change even the meekest of souls into raging bulls. I saw this shaping up the same way. He was out of control. On one hand, he used a threatening tone when Cassie didn't submit to his advances, on the other, he pledged his undying love for her. Can't have it both ways, Jack!

Jan had her determined face on and would not be thwarted by this pipsqueak. She was a formidable sight when angry and stood at military attention. She moved to stand directly in front of him, and then backed up a step, turning her head slightly aside. He stank of booze. I couldn't stand the smell from where I stood, so Jan must have caught a nasty whiff up so close. She raised her voice. "Mr. Sharples, you're cluttering up my kitchen and we all want you to leave. Especially Cassie who has no interest in a relationship with you. You should learn to take no for an answer."

I stood off to the side with Cassie right behind me. Griffith had blinked twice at Jan's charge, then turned away and began pacing about, or should I say lurching. His state of inebriation could lead to a tumble at any moment. He wove his way over to Cassie and made to put his arm around her. She cringed as he began to mumble. "All I want is a chance, Cashee. Once the theatre group casts for the play I'll get a part - you'll see, and you could do catering. We'd be able to work together. It would be perfect." His lopsided grin was anything but endearing.

Cassie, who tends to be a chatterbox, appeared spent. With legitimate reason. She'd been arguing with this undeniably handsome, but inebriated, young guy for a couple of hours. Her eyes beseeched me to get her out of this problem. The disturbance had escalated to the point of calling the police but wasn't something any of us wanted.

He was in no hurry to leave and while I wished Dianne was here already for moral support, as owner of Leven Lodge it would be up to me to handle this. I knew Jan would back me. Her clenched jaw and narrowed eyes told me as much. She inclined her head toward the full pot of coffee and then looked at Griffith. I got it.

I took a breath and steeled myself. Grabbing Griffith's hand, I pulled him away from Cassie and told him to sit down. To my relief he complied, although the chair threatened to topple as his unsteady weight dropped onto it.

Jan handed him a mug of coffee. A valiant effort to sober him up but he'll need more than that. I sat across from him. Jan and Cassie stood silently behind him, watching me. Great, all of a sudden, the show was mine.

"Griffith. Griffith! Pay attention. I don't know you at all, my concern here is for Cassie and this home. She's told you—more than once—to leave and as the owner here, I'm also telling you for the last time - hit the road! I'll even call a taxi to send you on your way. You didn't drive here in your condition, did you? No matter how busy the police are with their murder investigation, I'm sure they'd make the time to see about a restraining order." I opened my phone. "So, what's it to be? A taxi or call the cops for a restraining order?"

"Did I hear something about a restraining order?" Dianne, finally, stormed into the kitchen and went straight to stand in front of him.

She leaned down to stare him in the eye. "Right. What's it to be, handsome? We can call the cops to remove you bodily. I'm sure they'd love to throw you in a cell, charge you with harassment. Not to mention being drunk and disorderly. Or you can leave quietly. It's up to you."

Griffith's eyes blinked as if he'd seen an apparition. "Who the hell are you, gramma? Mind your own business. This is between Cassie and me."

Dianne turned to face us for a moment as if to say *Here we go,* before hooking her hand on the collar of Griffith's jacket. She kept her voice dead calm but brooked no-nonsense as she spoke right into his face.

"Listen to me, pal. There are four of us here and we're infuriated with you. So, if you don't leave quietly right now, with a promise to never return, we'll deal with you, which will be no problem, especially in your state. And we'll probably enjoy it. Got it?" She stopped to catch her breath and give him a chance to respond, which he didn't.

"Right, then. We have the cops on speed dial. And I bet if we hinted you might be connected to a murder investigation they'd be here in a flash and sort out the details later. Don't you know there's a murderer loose in Grant's Crossing?" She tightened the grip on his collar. "Speak up – what's it to be?"

I resisted the urge to clap my hands at Dianne's performance. I dared to hope she might have gotten through to the love-sick guy.

The would-be boyfriend had nothing to say about Dianne's command. He pushed himself away from the kitchen table and took a minute to steady himself. He looked at Cassie, smiled and uttered, "I *love* you, Cassie. I'll get a part in the play at the theatre, then you'll learn to love me. April underestimated my talents and should have cast me. A new director will see my talents."

He whipped the cap off his head and made a mock bow toward all of us. With a childish smile plastered across his face, he made for the hall doorway and left the kitchen. Dianne followed behind him and when we heard the front door bang shut, knew he was gone. Sighs of relief all around.

Once Dianne returned, with a triumphant smile and wiping her hands together, I gave my attention to Cassie, who had slumped onto a kitchen chair and held her head in her hands. I watched as she finally pulled herself together. She wiped away a few tears, and then straightened up.

Her voice was firm when she spoke. "I'm sorry you all got involved in that display, but I can assure you I didn't encourage him. Thanks for coming to my rescue." She cast her eyes downward in embarrassment "My father told me to dump him weeks ago, but I didn't see any harm in him. He's one of those guys, as Jan pointed out, who hasn't learned the word *no*. I've had coffee a couple of times with him just to be polite, but I've never seen him drunk before. Now I'll have to listen to my father say I told you so."

Cassie had some maturing to do, but I felt the crisis had passed. "I think Dianne put the fear of the cops in him. He probably won't bother you again. And Cassie? Your dad will be relieved. You're fortunate to still have a dad around who cares about you."

"Yeah, actually, my dad is pretty cool, thanks." She frowned. "I don't see Griffith giving up with the theatre group. He's convinced he's a good actor. You heard him, he believes he's talented, and maybe he is. So I'd better think twice about volunteering with them. Especially if he does get work there. I don't want to be worried about running into him." She sighed. "He also hangs with the other actors when they drop in at the pub. Oh! I just wish he'd move away!"

Jan made a move to lock the back door, part of her nightly ritual as she made final rounds of the lodge. "Cassie, all in all you handled things well but it's time to call it a day - for all of us. You're on duty to get breakfast started in the morning so I suggest you get to bed."

Dianne and I said goodnight to Cassie, and then to Jan, as she shooed us out of her kitchen. We knew she wanted to settle into her own routines before bed.

We kept our voices low, as we went up the stairs to the second floor where all was quiet. Early to bed for most of them but I didn't feel tired.

"Would you like a beer, Dianne? I've no tequila in my apartment but there should be a few beers Jeff left behind."

"An invitation I can't refuse. I'll tell you about my visit with Sherri."

I opened the door to my apartment, grabbed a couple of beers from the fridge, and told Dianne, "Sit wherever. We can catch Jan up tomorrow on Sherri."

We clinked our bottles and settled in for an hour or two of talk, where I learned more than I probably needed to about Sherri and Brock Wallis.

CHAPTER TWENTY-FOUR

Dianne

It had been another late night for Alysha. She won't be able to keep this up without paying a price. But she did want to hear all about Sherri and Brock Wallis. I tried to condense it as much as possible, but then of course we also discussed our concerns over Cassie and Griffith. Talk about not taking a hint. Griffith Sharples, while in no way resembling Sloane Jackson, had similar characteristics. Cassie's wise to keep her distance. His kind often spelled trouble in the end.

And we speculated on the outcome of Kyle Foreman's talk with the police. Alysha is anxious to build a clientele and having a client who wants to buy two properties is a big deal for her. I crossed my fingers in hopes all would work out for the best.

Alysha was right about one thing. The murder of April Lancashire had intruded on us enough. We weren't directly involved, so let the police do their thing. We parted company after midnight.

Then, this morning, she'd skipped breakfast with us and headed into work. Probably a much-needed distraction right now.

After breakfast had been cleared away, my peeps and I got to work. I offered to help the twins and Jan put up the Halloween decorations. Philip had even bagged a couple of decent sized pumpkins from a local farmer and showed interest in carving them. He was welcome to the sloppy task.

Alysha was a good sport over the decorations. I respected her desire to avoid the trick or treating and had offered to spend the evening with her. She'd seemed grateful for the suggestion, and we agreed to have a meal in her apartment and watch a couple of movies.

"Dianne!"

"Sorry, Rose. What did you say?"

"I asked if you would pass me the tape. Lily has managed to put a rip in one of the paper cut-outs."

As I handed over the roll of clear tape, I shot a smile of commiseration to Lily. Rose never hesitated to find ways to criticize her sister. Often uncalled for. "Here you are, Rose. This paper isn't the strongest, so I'd probably have torn it as well."

"I'd rather work with silk than this stuff." Rose ignored my comment and carried on with her taping. Sometimes she could be a first class...B.

Jan came into the dining room where all the spooky trappings were laid out. "Everything coming together?"

Sasitha brandished a toy straw broom in her direction. "I am not so sure this broom would make a good clean of your kitchen, Jan."

Jan chuckled. "I would have to agree with you. Ladies, Philip is up to his elbows in pumpkin pulp and seeds. Frank's been giving him a hand, and the pumpkins are almost ready to display." She looked over at Minnie, busy sorting candy into small treat bags. "He wanted me to ask you, Minnie, if you'd like to go around the back and be the first to see their handiwork?"

Minnie smiled. "I'll be right there."

A sense of contentment flooded through me as I looked at those around me. What a wonderful group of people and not for the first time did I appreciate being able to live here.

Bachan had gone into town, and Nina was upstairs writing. She'd tried to creep into the house undetected just before breakfast, but me and my early coffee fix meant I'd seen her, and I called her out on her behaviour before she slunk up the stairs. "Jan's right, you know. Why the heck don't you move into Bennett's?" She'd only shrugged and continued up to her room. I shook my head remembering her response.

"You okay, Dianne?" Jan had started to gather up the decorations for the veranda.

"Sorry. My mind's wandering all over the place this morning. Here, let me help you with those."

For the next hour or so we placed decorations on the veranda. Checking placement and ensuring the steps would still be safe for little feet. "So, who will be on candy detail?" I asked as we finished up.

"Rose volunteered right out of the gate, but Minnie also agreed to help. They can sort it out between them. I heard your offer to Alysha to spend the evening with her. Thank you. It's times like this she'll miss Jeff."

I brushed her off. No need to get all sentimental. "It will save me from duking it out with Rose and Minnie, right?"

"Whatever you say, Dianne." She gave me a quick hug.

I was spared further comment as Frank and Minnie came around the corner of the house. Frank pushed a wheelbarrow which held two impressive pumpkins, suitably carved. Placed at the foot of the stairs they finished off the decorations in style. I pulled out my phone for a couple of photos. If Frank had been holding a pitchfork they could be doubles for that old portrait of the stern farmer and his wife. Except for the smiles on both.

A satisfying day's work all around. And to keep us in a festive mood, I'd stocked the bar cart with a couple of special items. Pumpkin-spiced White Russian anyone?

The day's Happy Hour had been a success. In addition to the special White Russian, I also supplied the ingredients for a Pumpkin Pie Martini. Alysha seemed to quite enjoy the autumn inspired beverage. Nothing to do with Halloween at all.

Conversation during Happy Hour, and dinner, was light-hearted and the evening wound down without incident.

Alysha went straight up to her room after dinner, saying an early night was in store. Philip went about his alpaca chores, and with no Nina to spar with I retired to my room to catch up on email and read for a while.

I'd put my book down, reaching to turn out the light when my phone buzzed with an incoming text. From Alysha to let me know she'd heard from Kyle Foreman. Police had cleared him from anything to do with April Lancashire's murder. Good for him, but not so good for Sherri Wallis' deceased husband.

***

"Shopping list?" I enquired of Jan the next morning. She sat at the kitchen table, tapping a pencil against her chin, lost in thought. A lengthy list sat next to her coffee mug.

The temperature was predicted to be more like summer today and Jan had the kitchen windows open. A gentle breeze lifted leaves of the herbs she grew on a window ledge.

"Pull up a chair, Dianne. I'm glad to take a break." She pointed her pencil at the list. "Cassie has a couple of new dishes she wants to try, and of course, most items aren't staples in my pantry."

"Let me grab a coffee first. Anything happening with Griffith?"

"Thank goodness, he seems to have taken the hint. She said yesterday was the first day in weeks, she's had no phone call or text from him."

"What a relief." I said as I brought the coffee pot over to Jan and topped hers up.

A smile tugged at the corner of her mouth.

"What?"

"I'm pondering all the issues focusing on men we've been having here of late. Alysha and Jeff. You and Sloane. Now Cassie and Griffith. Is there a sign outside somewhere advertising space available for relationship problems?" The smile dropped a little. "I'm not being disrespectful when it comes to Sloane. You know that?"

"Water under the bridge. At least Nina keeps her man away from here. And Frank's only been beneficial to all of us. Especially Minnie.

So, they're not all bad. Certainly not on the level of Sloane. Although it turns my stomach to say I see similarities where Griffith is concerned."

Jan's face clouded. "I worry about that girl sometimes. I don't know if she's naturally naïve or if the pot she smokes has rattled her grey cells and common sense."

Now it was my chance to tease. "And were *we* brimming over with common sense at her age?"

Jan finished her coffee and stood. "Good point, Dianne. Now I need to finish this list and have chores to attend to. If you're not busy, could you run out to the barns and see how Frank's doing with winter preparation of the gardens?"

"I'll take a coffee refill with me."

I was glad she'd suggested the errand to see Frank. What a beautiful day. The sun's warmth on my face lifted my spirits. Leaves crunched beneath my feet, and I breathed in the fresh air of the countryside.

Frank and Philip worked side by side in the alpacas' barn. New beddings of straw were being laid and a general tidy-up was well in hand.

"Morning boys. Working hard?"

"Winter's coming, you know," said Philip. "Preparation is the key to survival. No hibernating."

There were times when Philip's ramblings sort of made sense.

"Yes, right you are, Philip. Frank, speaking of preparations. Jan's curious about progress on the gardens?"

"I'm on track and will have young Cory help out with some of the heavier chores this weekend. He's a good lad and not afraid of getting his hands dirty." He inclined his head in Philip's direction, who concentrated on spreading straw. "Can I have a word with you while he's busy?"

We walked out of the barn and into the sunshine. "Is there a problem with Cory?"

"Oh no. Not all. But mentioning him is what I want to talk about. See this?" He held out his hands, palms down. I'd never noticed the swollen joints before.

"That must be painful, Frank."

"Painful and a damn nuisance. I'm a hard worker." He frowned, unsure of how to continue.

"But?"

"It's not just my hands. My hips, my back, and... Oh, blast it. I hate getting old!"

He pulled a less than clean handkerchief from his pocket and rubbed his eyes. I never knew how to react when a man teared-up. Truthfully, I couldn't remember the last time I'd seen it.

"It's okay, Frank. What can I do?"

"I don't know how to approach Jan, but the day is fast coming when I'll be no use around here at all."

My heart hurt for him. The older I got, I became more aware of how time was often the enemy. I reached out a hand. "I'm sure it won't be a surprise to Jan. Now Cassie? Maybe." I tried to lighten the funk and was rewarded with a small smile.

"That gal has some growing to do. Her heart's in the right place."

"Let's focus on you, Frank. Would you like me to speak to Jan, or Alysha? You'll always be an asset to Leven Lodge. I'm sure something can be worked out. Trust me?"

"If you would, I'd be grateful. Thing is, if I can't work here anymore, it would mean I'd be away from Minnie as well."

Ah. The penny dropped. I understood his real worry. And it would be a concern for all of us. Frank was the steadying rock for Minnie. They talked and spent time together whenever he was on the property to work. And he often lingered at day's end to spend more time with her. Which got me to thinking.

"Frank. I've never asked, sorry. But I just assumed you have a home in Grant's Crossing?"

"I gave up keeping a proper home a long time ago. I have a couple of rooms over top one of the stores in town." He grimaced. "And the stairs to get up and down aren't fun anymore either."

"Don't you worry. Leave it to me. I'll talk to Jan and Alysha and see what we can do. You're as much part of this family as anyone."

Philip's voice reached us. "Frank. A lengthy discourse with non-labourers impedes our progress. Are you done?"

"Coming." He smiled at me. "I feel better now, thank you."

I wanted to say don't thank me yet but urged him back to his chores instead.

***

The day ended with a chat session. Alysha, Jan, and me in Jan's sitting room. Cassie had gone into town to help out at the Tavern so we could talk uninterrupted. After discussing the situation concerning her non-relationship with Griffith, I steered the conversation to Frank.

"No more coffee for me, thanks," I said to Jan as she offered another round.

Alysha stifled a yawn, prompting me to hurry things along. "I have something to talk to you both about. It's Frank."

"Oh?" Jan frowned. "Is there a problem?"

"Something with Minnie?" asked Alysha.

"Kind of all related. Here's the thing. He talked to me earlier today and asked if I'd have a word with you both."

I recapped his concerns and concluded by saying I'd more or less promised him we'd see what could be done.

"And what exactly did *you* have in mind?" Jan's teasing tone matched her bemused look.

Alysha, being much younger than Jan and me, perhaps didn't have the same empathy, but she was understanding when she spoke. "He's been invaluable to us. As a gardener, handyman, and so kind-hearted and perceptive when it comes to Minnie. Which I'm sure we all appreciate, right?"

"And he's been a loyal friend to me, and the lodge, over the years. A giving soul." Jan murmured more to herself than us. But I agreed with her, and Alysha.

I took a deep breath. "So, what can we do for him? He has no family to care for him and probably not a lot of savings. His options are limited." My mind had already formulated a plan, but it would have to come from Alysha and Jan - as in, let them think it's their idea.

"Leave it with me for a day or two. I may have an idea." Not like Jan to be cryptic, but I hoped she'd be on the same page as me.

"Yes," added Alysha. "Jan and I will brainstorm and see what we can come up with." She yawned again, this time not trying to hide it. "If you don't mind, ladies, I need to get some sleep."

We stood to leave, and Jan added a reminder. "Everyone ready for the Fall Fair this weekend?"

"I know I passed on going to it last year," said Alysha. "But yes, I'm looking forward to it. I'll be representing Bennett Howes' Real Estate for most of it but want to be a tourist as well. Jan, your pies are sure to do well in the contest. And Minnie has been knitting up a storm. What about you, Dianne?"

"I'm ready. The weather forecast is favourable for the next few days. I love the Fair and I know you will, too Alysha. You must have gone as a kid?"

"Yes, I did – some long-ago memories of those times. It will be different now, though. And you're still available to lend a hand where needed?"

I gave a mock salute. "Ready, willing and at your service."

Alysha and I made our way to the door, and I asked her, "Will you be down at breakfast tomorrow? It might be a good chance to ensure everyone else is ready?"

She frowned. "If I'm not there, I'll leave that task to you. Which reminds me. Jeff wants to borrow one or two of the alpacas for the petting zoo. I'd rather not be here when he comes round to get them."

Jan held her hand on the doorknob. A gentle suggestion we needed to get a move on. "Alysha, you don't need to deal with him. I'll take care of it if you like. For now, get some sleep. We have a busy time ahead, with the Fair and Halloween. Now, shoo!"

CHAPTER TWENTY-FIVE

Alysha

I'd only been at the office for an hour or two, answering emails and responding to queries for property showings, when a shadow tugged at the edge of my vision. I looked up from my desk to see Dianne hovering at the door, a mischievous smile etched on her face.

"Hey, are you working or putting on a worthy show?" She winked. "Wondered if you could get away for a bit?"

"Hey yourself. Trust me, this is not a show - I'm swamped with work right now but perhaps we can have a coffee when I'm finished. Almost lunch time anyway." I waved a hand over the files on my desk. "Lots of out-of-town clients in search of rentals or to buy. Grant's Crossing is growing in leaps and bounds."

"It's nice to hear positive news, isn't it?"

I smiled. "A good sign for me. I've managed to put all of them off for the moment. Instead, I've invited them to meet me at our real estate booth at the Fair tomorrow, or over the weekend, to talk business." I paused for a moment, unsure if I should share *insider information*. "I'm learning about business optics, don't you know? If the booth I'm working looks busy, that translates into an air of success and attracts more business. Or so says Bennett. I anticipate signing a few new clients. I guess he must be confident I'm up for the task, he's already said he won't be there all the time either. And Ernie has allergies so he's out. The hay would be too much for him."

"Good for you, kiddo. I'm proud of the way you've taken on this challenge."

Okay, I knew I grinned like a fool. "I'm having so much fun and it's exciting to see the town grow and develop."

Dianne gave me one of her best-behaviour smiles. "Can I wait here until you're finished? I'll be as quiet as a mouse."

I looked over at my friend and smiled back. "I won't be too long. Just a few more emails to answer. Help yourself to coffee in reception while you're waiting." I turned back to my computer and concentrated.

Dianne stayed true to her word. Not a peep from her as she silently disappeared from my office. I hurriedly finished my emails and as I shut down my computer Dianne exclaimed. "Come and look at this!"

I joined her at the office's large picture window. Over to the right of the town square stood the old cinema, still in the process of being converted into a theatre. Over a week now since the murder, the Countryside Players must be anxious to have the murder solved so the construction can continue and get them closer to an opening night.

"What are we looking at Dianne?" and then I saw what had her so bothered. Cassie and Griffith Sharples - disappearing from sight as they entered the building, ducking beneath the yellow police tape.

Dianne sucked air through her teeth. "What is that girl playing at? She's supposed to be running errands for Jan. Last minute things. Jan will be steamed. See, that's why I'm here. Cassie begged off running the errands for Jan, saying she needed to ready the pub's booth at the fair. If Jan learns she's decided to spend time with Griff instead, watch out!"

"But didn't we all agree she wanted nothing to do with him? Seems kind of strange, don't you think? Going inside there, with him?"

Dianne shrugged. "We'll see what Jan says later. However, I don't want Jan to be annoyed at me as well, so I'd better get cracking."

"And you want me to help you with these errands. Are you still afraid to go into the grocery store after your last encounter?" I loved teasing her.

"Pfft, as if. But should we do something about Cassie?"

Dianne. Asking me for advice? "Nothing, she's a grown woman. Maybe she changed her mind about him after all. If it doesn't happen at the lodge, I can live with it." I ran back to my office and grabbed my purse. "Let's go to that new place for coffee, *The Coffee Bean*, or whatever it's called. We can pick up Jan's supplies on the way home. And, if we're lucky, she'll cut a slice of her heavenly pie, just for us."

Dianne shot me a look but didn't question my response to Cassie and Griffith. Okay, I admit, it sounded callous, but really, we couldn't fight all her battles, could we? I parked the small tickle of guilt aside. "Hmm, okay, for you to talk about pie. I'm watching my waistline."

We said goodbye to Christine with instructions to send anything important to my inbox, and we went on our way.

***

The verdict's in. The new caffeine place is a winner. We're happy with the *Java Hut*, but it was about time the town had another option. And part of Grant's Crossing charm is its ability to withstand cookie-cutter franchises. So, another independent coffee shop was welcome - especially with the influx of visitors and hopefully, for me, new residents. I wanted to linger over my yummy cappuccino, but Dianne hustled me to the grocery store clutching her list.

Grocery stores have never been my thing. I'm not a cook unless it's to throw something into the microwave. A trait I shared with my shopping companion. It didn't take long to find what Jan needed but Dianne kept adding to the shopping cart with some personal items. The latest celebrity-fuelled magazine, hairspray, and a few treats she'd probably squirrel away in her bedroom. And bonus for both of us - no busybodies around to upset her over the Patels.

The sun was sliding lower in the sky when we finally made it back to the lodge. A white commercial van sat parked near the front steps, its driver heeding Jan's instructions on the loading of her special relishes, chutneys, and other preserves. She'd been working on these for weeks, along with a variety of pies, which were jammed into our commercial freezer in the kitchen. The pies would be transported tomorrow.

"Mind you don't break any of those jars!" I bet she would have preferred to load the van herself and had a hard time trusting the driver and his assistant to meet her standards of care.

She finally noticed us. "Oh, just in time ladies. I'm in need of a cup of tea and there's enough time before dinner chores to enjoy it. I'll put the kettle on."

But she didn't move, until the doors on the van closed and it drove away. We manoeuvred up the steps and around the pumpkins. Dianne made admiring comments on the decorations. And then we all moved inside and back toward the kitchen, where I hoped to find a pie with our names on it.

Jan switched on the kettle, looked at me and grinned. "I kept one pie back for a treat but don't let it spoil your dinner. Cassie has something special tonight." She frowned and glanced at the clock. "She's out right now but I'd hoped she'd be back by now to start preparations."

Dianne and I shared a glance. Her worried expression told me we had the same idea and better inform Jan we'd seen Cassie and Griff together.

"And that was a couple of hours ago. We thought it odd, but assumed she'd be back here by now." I knew Jan would be annoyed to learn Cassie had gone off with Griffith.

She slammed the lid on the teapot with a little more force than necessary. "Is she still smoking joints then? She must be because her judgement's gone to pieces if she's with him. She swore she was giving up pot - and Griffith!"

Not much chance Cassie would willingly give up the weed. Probably best not to share that with Jan, no need to provoke her further. "She's on her last legs with me. I need staff I can depend on. She's got one more hour to show her face. Without Griffith Sharples, either!"

While Jan made our tea and sliced some pie I whispered to Dianne, "Do you think we should just wait a bit longer to see if she gets back here? I have a bad feeling that she's this late." The guilt I'd pushed aside had grown.

"I'm thinking the same thing. Let's wait a bit longer, and then if she's not back, we could go into town?"

I could only nod in agreement as Jan placed a plate with pie in front of me. So, while I tucked into a slice of delicious peach pie, Jan and Dianne drank tea. We all seemed to be lost in our own thoughts, but Jan's face told me she was growing more vexed by the minute.

The last morsel of pie disappeared from my plate, and as I got ready to leave, I decided to test the waters with Jan. "I'm sure she'll be here soon, with an explanation."

Jan's response was a tight-lipped *hmmm*.

"Right, I'll head over to the barn and see how Cory is managing without Jeff. You know, I like that kid." My offer softened the furrows on Jan's face, as she responded. "You'll find they're minus two alpacas. Jeff was here at the crack of dawn to grab them for the petting zoo."

I'd forgotten about that for the moment, and the mention of Jeff's name still gave me an unpleasant jolt. "Thanks for dealing with him this morning. Did he take Larry and Moe?"

"Yes, he did. Gillian was with him. They said the boys would be brought home late Sunday after the Fair ends."

Dianne offered to give Jan a hand in the kitchen, and I assured them both I'd be back in a few minutes to see if Cassie had returned.

***

Cory was in his element looking after the alpacas and he confidently asserted he'd be able to settle them for the night as Frank had gone home. "I'm not sure where Philip is. He went to the paddock, muttering something about taking a roll call?"

"Don't worry about Philip. I'm sure he'll check back later. Speaking of Frank, this gives me a chance to talk with you." I must have scared him, because his crestfallen face showed he thought bad news was coming in his way. "Hey, it's all good where you're concerned. You may not have noticed, but the heavy work Frank does around here is growing more difficult for him. So... we're hoping, you might be willing to take on some of his chores. Think you can fill the gap?"

Cory couldn't keep the grin off his face – pushing the frown away. "Awesome! Shouldn't be a problem for me. I work well with Philip and he's teaching me about animal husbandry. Which helps me gain practical experience for later on! Thank you, Ms. Grant! I won't let you down."

His enthusiasm was contagious and like Dianne, I also felt compelled to help him reach his goals. "Excellent! We have a win-win situation. But, as Dianne would say, your schoolwork still comes first. One more thing. You must be upfront with us, got it? Don't be afraid to ask for help."

"I won't. And... I really like working here. Everyone makes me feel at home."

Not wanting this to dissolve into a sentimental moment, I held out my hand to shake his. "Deal then. Now, you need to get back to work, right?"

He nodded so hard I thought his neck would snap, but it made me smile. I walked over to pet the crias. Ryker and Roxy were in capable hands with Cory and Philip. A few more weeks and they'd be weaned from their mothers' care.

I said my goodbyes and strolled back to the house with my fingers crossed that Cassie had returned. Autumn's darkness had crept in, and the air was crisp and cool. Perfect running weather. With any luck I might get back to my running routine once the fair wrapped up.

Entering the kitchen, I heard Jan banging pots and grumbling to herself. So, unlike her and meant I didn't need to ask about Cassie. Dianne must have finished helping her and left because I didn't see her.

Jan swivelled around when she saw me, her face stony. "Don't ask. She's still not here. Glad I have backup dinners in the freezer."

I knew it! And now the guilt was full blown. "This is more than annoying. Listen, I'll get Dianne and we'll go back to the theatre. Maybe she's still there with lover boy. Though why they'd hang out there I don't know."

Dianne came flying down the stairs, car keys in hand. "I heard you talking with Jan. Let's go. I don't like this either. I never liked the vibes from Griffith from the first time I laid eyes on him."

We made for the front door, Jan following behind. "You think there might be something wrong, then? Now I'm worried. Be careful and keep in touch, and when you get back there'll be lasagne waiting. I've more than enough to keep the hungry hordes satisfied." She tried to smile, but I could see anxiety written all over her.

We made the trip to the theatre in record time. Streetlights were on but the theatre was in darkness. A few people were out and about but it was dinner time for most and the stores were closing. Only the pub at the other end of the street was humming with those in search of a meal and a drink.

We parked on the other side of the street and Dianne killed the engine. She drummed her fingers on the steering wheel. I looked at her profile. Woman on a mission. "Are you ready? It's probably locked but they went in the front door so..."

"Let's go." We ran across the road to the building, and I tried opening the door we'd seen them enter. The door resisted my initial attempt, but when I put my weight behind the effort it opened easily. So much for security.

And then I hesitated. "What if there's cameras? We should call the cops. Last thing we need is to be arrested for break and enter, or trespassing."

"Chill. If we don't find them here, we'll leave as quietly as we came. Okay?"

"And if we do find them? What then?"

"We'll cross that bridge when we come to it. Let's be quiet though. You never know - there might be a security guard or something."

I was beginning to have doubts about this venture but decided to let her take the lead. For now.

We were in the lobby and ticket office area. Between the drywall dust and musty smell my nose tickled with a growing need to sneeze.

Dianne held her phone in front of her, which gave us a small beam of light to follow. An exit sign glowed faintly so at least I knew there had to be electricity on. I kept my hand on her arm as we groped our way to the auditorium area of the theatre.

She halted and gripped my arm. "Shh! Listen. What's that? Voices?"

We'd stopped outside a large, and heavy, pair of swing doors, and now I heard voices, muffled, on the other side. I held my breath as she gently pushed one door open, and we moved through the entrance to crouch down behind the back row of seats. Construction material was everywhere; untouched in the last week since the police had closed off the theatre to investigate. I peeked over the top of the seat back and could see a spot, cleared to store workers' supplies. Police tape sectioned off one area. If only Jeff hadn't been so eager to drop off material for props and sets, he'd never have been involved in this. I shivered as I realized it was where April had been murdered.

But it was the beam of light, a spotlight, shining on centre stage which grabbed my attention and made my stomach tighten. Dianne managed to stifle a gasp. She didn't need to tell me to keep quiet.

Cassie! And Griffith - shouting in her face. It was hard to see from my vantage point, but one arm was above her head and when she moved the spotlight bounced off something shiny. A handcuff?

I hissed in Dianne's ear. "She's handcuffed to the scaffolding! Holy crap. What do we do?"

I probably didn't need to worry whether Griffith would hear me. His tirade came across loud and clear. As did Cassie's sobs and pleas to be let go.

Dianne pointed to her cell phone. "No service in here. We need the cops."

I couldn't respond, paralysed by the outpouring of anger and hate directed at Cassie - all too familiar to me when I'd been held captive.

He ranted and railed over the never-ending string of disappointments he'd endured in his life. Never being given a chance. Never taken seriously.

"I thought things would be different with you, Cassie. I loved you from the first moment I saw you. But you couldn't give me a chance, could you!" The words he spat were full of venom and fury. "You and April. Cut from the same cloth the pair of you. She never gave me a chance either. When this place is up and running, I'll get a part. The lead! Why not?" He ran out of steam and slumped at Cassie's feet. "You'll see. Then you'll be proud of me, won't you?"

Her sobs intensified. "Please Griff. Let me go. I think... I think you need some help."

He jumped to his feet again. "Help? That's what she said, too. Stupid bitch. Well, I showed her, didn't I?"

We weren't close enough to see, but Cassie had to be crying. He swore her tears had no effect on him. "April wanted to cry, too, I could tell. And now you're rejecting me as well." He softened his voice and began stroking the side of her face. "We could have had something special." His voice dropped even lower, and I couldn't make out his words.

I nudged Dianne. "Go and get the cops. Maybe your phone will work in the lobby or go outside. We need help."

Her piercing gaze underscored my indecisiveness when she whispered harshly. "You're not going to do anything stupid are you?"

"I don't have a plan if that's what you mean. Go already!" She waffled and I pushed at her. "It's better we split up. I'll stay and keep an eye on her."

When she moved away, I was surprised she'd listened to me, but I could feel the adrenaline pushing me to action. I knew what it felt like to be in Cassie's situation, and I had to do something!

I watched Dianne as she crept toward the swing door. Damn! This time it creaked when she opened it. Then she was gone. I turned back to look at the stage.

He must have heard the door and turned to face the seats, sweeping a flashlight across the empty spaces. I ducked before it revealed my position.

"Who's there? Show yourself."

My heart hammered in my chest. Banking on the assumption he didn't have a gun, I stood up and began a cautious move in his direction. I willed my nerves to behave and tried to speak in a normal voice.

"I didn't know you were rehearsing for a role, Cassie. Or are you helping Griff? I can see you both have talent. What's the role you're trying out for, Griff?" I talked and kept moving forward, buying time. By now Dianne would have help on the way.

"Stop! Stay where you are. This is a closed set. You're not part of it, and not welcome."

I ignored his command and kept walking until I reached the stairs at the side of the stage. I needed to focus on him but stole a glance at Cassie. Her split lip and swollen eyes spoke to the abuse she'd suffered at Griffith's hand. Anger bubbled up inside me, but I needed to contain it.

"Griffith. Come on now. You know you can't win anyone's love this way? Perhaps you could release Cassie and then the three of us can sit and talk. I'll be happy to show Cassie that you're a decent person and you make a good couple. Right?"

He glared at me, and I pulled Cassie into the pretence. "Isn't that right, Cassie? We can all sit and talk. Maybe you've been mistaken about Griffith all along." Thank God, she got it.

After a couple of sniffles, she uttered an almost inaudible, "Yes, I'd like that."

I knew I'd keep playing for time as long as I had to. Griff was becoming more unhinged by the minute. He'd begun to roam around the stage, swinging his arms as if to embrace everything around him.

"And Griff, I'm staying put because I also want to hear about the plays you've acted in. I'll even put a good word with the new director. I'm sure you'll be cast in a perfect role."

He stopped his pacing and stared at me. "Why should I believe you?"

"Because I have pull here in Grant's Crossing, that's why. And I recognize talent when I see it!"

That was enough for this ego-driven and frustrated actor to start talking about himself instead of Cassie. He flung himself around the stage. He recited lines from works not familiar to me and ran the gamut of body language. Which meant he ignored both Cassie and me. Engrossed in his maniacal performance he wasn't aware of the movement I noticed off to one side of the stage. I kept my eyes on Griff as Dubois and another uniformed cop rushed from behind a curtain and tackled Griff to the ground.

I finally began to breathe normally, and I rushed to Cassie. "See if he has a key on him for these!"

Dubois uttered the words I was grateful to hear. "Griffith Sharples, I'm arresting you on suspicion in the death of April Lancashire." He patted the pockets of the subdued man and produced a key.

Cassie was soon released and collapsed against me, sobbing. "I've never been so scared, Alysha. Thank you for rescuing me."

I stroked her hair and handed her a tissue. "Don't thank me, you still have to face Jan for being late. That's what you should be scared about!"

The small smile my comment elicited told me Cassie would be okay. A paramedic had come forward to double-check, followed by Dianne.

As the paramedic cared for Cassie, I felt a tap on my shoulder. Dubois had handed over the prisoner to his colleague and left me with a parting shot.

"Ms. Grant, we must stop meeting like this!"

CHAPTER TWENTY-SIX

Dianne

Around the dining room table, mouths were agape, and not a whole lot of breakfast was being consumed as Cassie finished yet another recount of last evening's events at the theatre. Even Philip appeared captivated by her tale.

Her split lip had started to heal, and she seemed none the worse for what had been a close call. Or maybe she'd started the day with a little help. Whatever the reason, I'd endure her chattering. Especially when I considered the alternative.

Jan, on the other hand, had taken on the anxious energy Cassie was known for. She had no time for small talk this morning and seemed distracted. Probably, because Grant's Crossing Fall Fair was upon us.

Alysha pushed away from the table and trailed after Jan into the kitchen. She and I agreed to offer Jan our help wherever needed.

Alysha had been given a free day from normal real estate duties, and the High School would let out just after lunch, meaning Cory would be around to lend a hand as well. He'd never participated in the event and was excited to be included.

I grabbed my empty coffee mug and followed Alysha's lead. When I entered the kitchen, she was doing her best to lend a hand by loading the dishwasher.

"What can I do, Jan?" I reached for the dishcloth and made to tackle the dirty pans soaking in the sink.

"Much appreciated, Dianne. It should be Cassie doing this. Today of all days! Plus her responsibilities with her father's tavern presence at the fair."

"We'll get through it, Jan. Don't worry. Dianne and I can clean up in here if there are things you need to do for the fair."

"The worst of it has been taken care of." Jan looked at both of us. "I haven't even asked either of you how you slept after yesterday's excitement. I knew Griffith wasn't quite right, but never pegged him as a murderer."

Alysha closed the door of the dishwasher and pushed buttons. "On that score, he had us all fooled, I guess. I don't like to think how things might have ended out if Dianne and I hadn't gone after her." She exhaled a big sigh. "When Dianne and I finished talking with Dubois last night, he said Griffith wasn't saying a word until he had a lawyer. Even if he's not involved with April Lancashire's murder, being charged with assault and forcible confinement should clip his wings for a while."

I turned from the sink of soapy water. "That reminds me. I need to give Sherri a call later. She'll be relieved to know this might clear her husband of any suspicion. Too little and too late for him, though."

Cassie sailed into the kitchen with a tray of dirty dishes. "Too late for who? Oh, dishwasher's on? These'll be for the next load, then."

Alysha took the tray from her and began to unload it. "Cassie. How are you doing today? Are you going to have to speak to the police again?"

Her face lit up. "Oh yes. Steven—that is DC Dubois—promised he'd drop by later to go over the details again. He looked after me well last night and made sure I was okay. I've never talked that much with him before. I don't see him as much of a social person. Never seen him in the Tavern. Other than on police business. Oh, I could invite him for a meal there – on the house. To thank him for his kindness."

No more Griffith Sharples on her radar, perhaps.

Jan's mouth worked, trying to get a word in edgewise. "Take a breath, girl. All in good time. Now then. One last check." She turned to Alysha and me. "Includes you both as well. There's no formal dinner this evening. Most of us will be at the Fair in one capacity or another from now till Sunday. So, Cassie and I have filled the fridge with meals that only need to be heated in the microwave for anyone who wants. Toast or cereal for breakfast. Got it?"

"Aye, aye, Captain." I smiled at our fearless leader. "And I'm thinking you'd prefer to be heading over to the fairgrounds now yourself. So let Alysha and I clean up here. You and Cassie take care of business over there. We'll be along later when the gates open."

Jan faced Alysha. "Don't you need to be there early for the real estate booth?"

She shook her head. "Bennett said yesterday he'd be there first thing today and the booth will be set up. Not much to do I would say. Some pamphlets to put out and he had a poster made. I think he's playing on my good side, so I'll work the crowds when I'm there and he'll sit at the table. So, Dianne's right. Go take care of what you're itching to do! And I'll make sure everyone knows it's a fend-for-yourself weekend around here. We'll see you in a few hours."

Jan had untied her apron before Alysha finished speaking. "Let's go, Cassie. I have displays to set up, but you have food and drink to stock and prepare."

And then they were gone, leaving a vacuum of silence behind, until Alysha chuckled. "Should we warn Dubois?"

***

You couldn't ask for a better weather forecast. Bright blue skies, warm temperatures. Wouldn't be too many more like this before winter made an appearance.

We arrived at the fairgrounds; grateful Alysha had reserved parking. The parking lot was already full, and more cars were arriving in a steady stream.

The fairgrounds were more than one hundred years old. The main building had been built about sixty years ago and had been made to resemble a barn structure familiar to so many in the area. The huge interior housed animal pens on one side, displays of handmade crafts and local businesses down the centre aisles and food related booths on the other side.

Picnic benches and other seating had been made available for enjoying pub grub, sandwiches, hot dogs, and beaver tails. The Crossings Tavern had the largest venue and with a liquor license would probably enjoy a brisk trade. My parched throat said I'd be paying a visit before long.

Outside the main building, smaller craft areas and ticket booths had been set up. An impressive array of farm machinery stood at the ready for inspection. A decent sized carnival area with a small Ferris wheel and other rides would keep the kids interested. Stacks of hay bales sported signs advertising various attractions and local business sponsors.

Dust drifted all around us, along with ever-present bits of straw. Cows lowed and horses neighed, competing with kids' shouts and squeals of excitement. Even though I'd been to fall fairs dozens of times over the years, I still found myself caught up in the atmosphere.

"It hasn't changed much since I was here as a kid." Alysha had stopped outside the door reserved for participants. She stood and looked out over the ring where horses, sheep and other cattle would be judged. "I remember the Merry-Go-Round. My grandfather rode with me when I was small, but I'll never forget the first year he let me sit on the horse by myself. So long ago now."

"And today you're making new memories, participating from the other side. C'mon, let's get inside. I like to check out the food items before they disappear."

***

Nothing like homemade cookies - which would be going straight to my room. The variety of jams and jellies in my shopping bag would be shared in Leven Lodge's kitchen. Before stopping for a glass of my favourite brew I'd wandered around.

Alysha stood tall. Well, as tall as someone her height can, in front of the display for Bennett Howes' Real Estate. She handed out business cards with enthusiasm. I saw the display of knitted baby sweaters from Minnie, whom I'd bumped into while she took in the sights with Frank on her arm.

Brodan Construction had a designated booth, but nothing yet was set up. Not a promising sign and reminded me I need to talk with Sherri. I'd circle back around. Maybe she wasn't planning on being there till tomorrow.

I didn't linger at the petting zoo area. Our two alpacas were settled in their pen, but no sign of Jeff, or Gillian. And while piglets were cute, all I saw was future bacon.

Tomorrow would be a busy day. Lots of animals to be judged. Competition might be friendly but those who ended up with ribbons enjoyed special status. Jan would be on pins and needles until results were in for all the competing pies and other food entries. There could be no doubt Grant's Crossing enjoyed a bountiful harvest on many levels.

I made my way to the Crossings Tavern area. "Hi, Cassie. I'll have whatever you have on draught. Business doing okay?" Cassie offered me a quick greeting. She was being kept busy behind the counter for her father's pub. I handed over payment, disappointed to receive a can of beer. I should have remembered they wouldn't have draught available. I prefer not to drink from a can, so Cassie gave me a plastic cup, which I took to the nearest bench. Time for some people-watching.

I waved to a few familiar faces and then busied myself with my phone when I spied Janice O'Hare and Marjorie Bell. I needn't have bothered hiding, they were so caught up in their chattering and finger pointing they marched right past me without a second glance. I'd have to get over myself where they were concerned, but not today.

Phone in hand, I called Sherri, but it went to voicemail. "Hi Sherri. It's Dianne. Thought I'd check on how you're doing. Call me when you get a chance, or I might see you at the fair."

Time was getting on. The midway closed at 11:00, but most of the displays and booths started packing up just after nine.

I was tempted to have another beer and sit, but I also thought I'd better wander around again and see how Jan had fared and if Alysha was ready to call it quits for the day. As I stood, a hand touched my shoulder. "Got your message."

I turned to see Sherri, who looked a lot better than she had in recent days. At least her hair was tidy, and she'd made an effort with make-up. "I should have been here earlier, but as I was leaving, the cops showed up. Told me about the arrest." She almost smiled. "I can't tell you how relieved I am this takes the suspicion away from Brock. Police said you had a lot to do with the murderer's arrest. You and the owner of Leven Lodge."

I stood taller and threw my shoulders back, as if I could conquer anything. I let her assumption that Griffith was the murderer pass uncontested. Far as I knew it hadn't been confirmed one way or the other, but in the meantime, I accept the accolade. "I, that is, Alysha and I, couldn't believe our timing. In hindsight I think adrenaline took over. We were pretty shaken when the dust settled, but if we hadn't gone looking for Cassie, there's no telling what might have happened." I pointed to the other side of the bench. "Sit for a minute. Want a drink or something to eat?"

She shook her head. "No. Can't stop. I want the display all ready to go for the morning, but thought I'd say hi and to thank you for helping Brock get his name cleared."

She went on her way, and I made my way over to Alysha. The smile on her face spoke volumes.

"Dianne! Bennett will be pleased. I've signed three prospective buyers! And this is only the first night!"

"Good for you, kiddo."

"I'm not surprised at all, little one." Jan had joined us - her smile equal to Alysha's. I couldn't resist a tease

"And do you have any wares left to sell tomorrow, Ms. Young?"

"Well, if I run out, I have orders for more! It's only the first night, but I can't help noticing a lot of new faces this year."

"Visitors, or participants," I asked.

"Oh, visitors for sure," answered Alysha. "I've been talking to so many who are coming to the area or considering it. The Rivermill Resort has been mentioned more than a few times."

"So, for better or worse, Grant's Crossing is an up-and-coming community. Alysha, you must promise me to do all you can to ensure we never lose the essence of what makes this a charming town."

"Jan, you have my word. I share your concerns. In fact, you may have inspired me to become more involved with the community. Best way to make a stand is from within."

"Warrior women!" I laughed. "Are we ready to call it a night?"

Before either of them answered, we were distracted by a flash of vibrant orange. The oversized shawl flowed behind Nina who marched toward us. If frothing at the mouth wasn't a kind description for a human being, I'd say that's what I saw. Being upset was too mild a description.

Her face was a blotchy red, and mascara had smudged itself well below its original application. "Is he here?"

I held up a hand. "Whoa...slow down a minute. Who do you want?"

Her eyes narrowed and if her lipstick-less lips were pressed any tighter they'd disappear. She hissed. "Mr. Bennett two-timing Howes, that's who."

I became aware of a circle of fascinated faces around us – including the witchy pair I'd avoided earlier. For a moment I enjoyed knowing I wasn't the centre of their gossip machine.

Jan and Alysha had moved closer to Nina, on either side of her. Jan, so well-known in the community, made it clear folks should move on. "Nothing to see here, other than a need for privacy. Please."

Her gentle voice carried an air of authority I'd never have. I'd been ready to shriek at everyone to clear off. Jan's way was preferable.

We moved Nina off to the side and found a quiet corner. She trembled with anger, and I feared the volcano would blow again any second.

"Okay, what's going on? What happened?" I couldn't wait for anyone else to start the questions.

"He's about to learn I won't put up with his... his behaviour. No second chances where I'm concerned. Men!" She was literally spitting mad. Alysha handed me a tissue.

Then Nina took a breath. "I'm sorry, Alysha. I know he's your boss and I hope this won't affect your working for him, but I'm through!"

"Nina. Calm down. Don't worry about my work. Tell us what happened?"

Nina's shoulders finally relaxed, and her breathing slowed. "I'm sorry, chickees. Didn't mean to come flying at you all like this. Dianne, you'll probably understand this better. When a man cheats and thinks nothing of it, it says all you need to know about their character."

Oh, brother. What a familiar story. She was right, Jan wouldn't be able to relate. But Alysha coughed to get attention. "Um, Nina. Hello? I'm a member of that club now, right?"

Nina smirked. "Sorry, chickie. For a moment I forgot, but you're right. You've still got years ahead to find the right one. But for me, game over. I'm done. Hemingway's a much better companion... in most areas."

"And we won't touch that line, will we?" My comment brought a lighter outlook to the group.

Nina grew serious. "Needless to say, Jan, you can consider this my notice to vacate. I had planned to stick around for the Countryside

Players to get up and running. Thought I had a worthy reason to stay here, but I need to go. I'll be gone after Halloween if not before. I did promise to lend a hand here, which I will keep, and then I'd like to treat all my friends at the lodge to a night out, or order-in. A night off for you and Cassie. To thank you for the hospitality."

"Oh, Rose and Lily won't be happy. Will you still work on their book?" Jan's concern, naturally, settled more for the twins than Nina.

"No worries there, Jan. I've got the outline complete, just have to put it into words. I'll keep in touch with them. Too much invested in it to quit now. Unlike Bennett!"

And we were back full circle. I raised an eyebrow in Alysha's direction, and she took charge. "Let's leave it there, okay? Things might look different in the morning. I said, different, not better, Nina."

The building was almost empty, so thankfully no more audience. Time to put this day to bed.

CHAPTER TWENTY-SEVEN

Alysha

Not for the first time I pondered on the different personalities I interact with, both in my day-to-day life here at the lodge and my clients at work. To say they make life interesting would be an understatement. Most of the residents of the lodge were involved in the fair and I anticipated I'd meet a few new clients at the real estate booth. Keeps me on my toes and I wouldn't have it any other way. As I sipped my coffee on the balcony, I savoured the view over the meadows while I contemplated the single life without Jeff.

My plan? Embrace all Grant's Crossing has to offer. I'm determined to make my mark as a realtor and become more involved in the community. Bennett might make a formidable competitor in my future, but I'd give him a run for his money. And I'll always be grateful for his mentoring.

I shook myself out of my reverie when the intercom squawked. "Alysha are you there?"

"Just finishing my morning coffee, Jan. What's up? I'm in realtor mode and ready to leave." I put my coffee cup in the sink.

"Good, because we're waiting for you here. The gang is ready to set off. Better come and claim your seat or you'll be walking to the fairgrounds."

"On my way." I smiled at Jan's comments. Her commanding-officer persona often covered up unease or anxiety, although at times I think she enjoys it.

I grabbed my jacket and purse and ran down the stairs where I found a group of chattering residents. Anxious to get going, their excitement was palpable - and contagious.

Frank fussed over Minnie who could hardly contain herself. She'd been so anti-social over the years, I couldn't imagine how she'd manage. Except she had Frank to watch over her. "Do you have a warmer sweater, love? It is October, you know." His care of her was touching.

The twins, as often the case, dressed in opposite fashion. Rose dressed as if for a garden party. Probably better suited to springtime rather than fall, but I wasn't going to make a comment. Flowery dress and large hat in contrast to her twin, who wore a quilted jacket and comfy slacks. A better choice in my opinion.

"You're well prepared for the day, Lily." She rewarded me with a grateful smile. I assessed the group and made a suggestion about transportation. "Why don't I take my car, Jan, as I've been given reserved parking courtesy of Bennett." I looked around. "Where's Dianne? Isn't she coming with us? I heard her say she'd be glad to help Sherri Wallis, or anyone else as needed."

Jan gave me the once over. "Glad you've sensible shoes on today, Alysha. Those spiked heels you wear for work are hazardous when crossing a field. Yes, you're right about Dianne. She's left already."

"Wait for me!" Cassie came running from the kitchen. "I just had a phone call from Steven about Griffith."

Jan and I froze. I waited to hear the words confirming he was the confirmed murderer of April Lancashire.

"Steven says new evidence has come to light and he's not suspected of the murder, but the assault charges stand."

I groaned inwardly. This meant Brock Wallis hadn't been cleared after all. I wondered if his widow knew already.

Cassie yammered on about taking the call and worrying we'd leave without her – thoughts of Griffith apparently no longer an issue with her.

"As if we could forget you. Come along. You come with me" said Jan, "and mind the pies in the back seat! Alysha will take the twins, plus Frank and Minnie."

"And Nina?" I asked. "I guess she went on ahead as well to set up her booth for her book selling?"

Jan hustled everyone out the door but held back to make a comment just for my ears. "I'm disappointed this murder hasn't been solved yet. But at least Griffith will be out of the picture as far as Cassie is concerned. And as for Nina? She hasn't left yet. I'm not sure what the problem is with our resident diva but she's not happy with the booth she's been allotted. I believe she's arriving later once she's walked the mutt. I mean Hemingway. At least she has the common sense not to bring it along today."

"Oh dear, I'll check into it when we arrive. I thought Bennett oversaw booth allocations. But maybe her bad humour is more of a reflection on what she's learned about him."

Jan frowned. "And on that subject, I'll keep my comments to myself."

We moved to get into our respective cars. At the last minute, the Patels came out to the veranda, promising to come along later in the day. That left Philip in charge of the remaining alpacas and to keep an eye on the house. Cory was to meet us there as well and would be kept busy with the livestock displays. Sound experience for him.

"Seat belts on?" I teased. Frank sat between the twins in the back, while Minnie rode next to me which made me glad it was only a few minutes to our destination. As I turned the ignition, I felt excited, but strangely at peace, anticipating the potential of new business opportunities for Grant's Crossing.

***

Once inside the main building, Jan, Cassie, and I headed off to our respective areas and prepared for the day.

Rose and Lily were free to wander around. I'd just finished lining up business cards and posting a couple of new photo listings when they stopped by. I don't know where Lily's interests lay for the fair, but Rose obsessed over fabrics and creativity. "Oh, and I saw Minnie over by the Knitting Guild's exhibit. She couldn't stop inspecting her contributions to win a ribbon." She paused for effect. "As if she has a chance."

"Rose, don't be so mean. Minnie has been knitting for years. What she's made is every bit as good as anything else there."

Well done, Lily. She didn't often call Rose on her airs of superiority, and I resisted the urge to compliment her. Instead, I reflected on the recent positive changes in Minnie's demeanour, but before I could say a word, Frank sauntered over with a cardboard tray full of coffee cups. Thank heavens he was so thoughtful. I doubted I'd get away for a coffee for a while - especially after seeing the long line-up to get in. We were in for a busy day!

Leven Lodge was well represented for the weekend, and I'd be surprised if Jan had any of her pies left by Sunday evening. They'd soon disappear. No one had mentioned seeing Nina and I was curious to know if she'd arrived. Her booth was around the corner from me, so I couldn't easily see.

I checked my watch. Bennett should have been here by now. We'd agreed to spell each other an hour at a time, and I anticipated playing visitor around the rest of the fairgrounds, when not engaged with prospective clients. I stood out front of the table, handing brochures and business cards to interested fair goers when I got a tap on my shoulder.

"Bennett, glad you're here. It's starting to get busy, and I worried you were held up at the office." His usual gregarious nature was absent, and he appeared distracted.

"No, no. Sorry to be late. Something came up I needed to deal with and I've a few things on my mind." Then he smiled. "Good turnout so far, I see. Excellent! I'll take over now if you want a break. You'll be back in an hour, right? Oh, and by the way, have I told you how happy I am with the work you're doing? You will go far. I knew the minute I met you that you'd be what Grant's Crossing needed."

"Thank you, Bennett. I appreciate it." Compliments unnerve me, so I tried to change the topic. I picked up on a level of despair his babbling couldn't disguise. The break-up with Nina perhaps had shaken him, but that wasn't a subject I'd mention. "I'd like to wander around for a bit but will be back."

"Go ahead, I'll man the fort."

Truth be told for the first time since I'd known Bennett, I was glad to be out of his company. The vibe he gave off made me uncomfortable. Or was I being too sensitive to anyone dealing with a breakup. I hoped he'd be more settled by the time I returned.

I smiled at him, saved from further comment when my phone rang. I walked away to answer Dianne's call. "Hi. You got an early start on the rest of us this morning. Is everything okay?"

It didn't sound like she'd heard the news about Griffith. For now, I'd play innocent and not mention anything.

"All good. Any chance you'd come by to meet Sherri? I'm with her at the Brodan Construction display. She's facing the front entrance."

"On my way." I had to weave my path through dozens of people, and passed Jan's booth, but didn't stop to say hi because she was engaged in conversation with potential customers. Potential? Who am I kidding! Anyone who knows Jan knows her pies are legendary. I walked and talked. "I'm going to need your advice on something or rather someone. Can you get away? I need to talk to you about Bennett and I'd rather speak to you without an audience."

"Sounds intriguing. Is he the new man in your life?" Dianne started to giggle.

"Oh, you. Don't be silly." I disconnected when she came into view.

"Here she is now." Dianne spoke to the attractive woman beside her. She wore a white construction hat and had dressed in a semi-casual business jacket. This must be Sherri Wallis. "Sherri, this is my good friend, Alysha Grant. Alysha - Sherri."

"Good morning, ladies." I shook Sherri's hand, and offered my condolences, which she'd probably heard numerous times. Her automatic thank you confirmed my hunch when she quickly changed the subject. I could relate wanting to avoid painful subjects.

Her face brightened when she asked, "Are you a Grant as in Grant's Crossing? My family's been here for decades and have long been acquainted with them in the past. My grandfather was a carpenter, and I believe he may have been instrumental in the renovation of the farmhouse. Estelle and Wilf Grant?"

She seemed genuinely interested - not making small talk to divert attention from her recent loss. And confirmed neither she nor Dianne knew Griffith was no longer suspected in the murder. I decided they wouldn't hear it from me, and commented on my family history instead.

"Yes, I am. Estelle and Wilf were my grandparents, and I own that farmhouse now, except it's now known as Leven Lodge. Small world."

"One of the things we like about Grant's Crossing, isn't it, Alysha?" Dianne had stayed out of the conversation, but true to form, let us know she was still part of it. "That small-town feel with a solid community spirit."

The community spirit angle might be a stretch where Dianne was concerned, and I wondered if she was trying to score brownie points with Sherri. Whatever. I nodded at her but spoke to Sherri. "In addition to running Leven Lodge, I've also taken up real estate now. You know, clients often ask for referrals for a contractor." I paused for a moment. "Why don't we help each other? May I take a few of these?" I reached for several of her business cards displayed behind her.

I was repaid with a warm smile. "How kind of you. Absolutely. Take as many as you like and if you give me some of yours, I'll be sure to pass them along."

I gave myself a mental pat on the back, gaining more confidence promoting myself. But time to steer away from business. "So, is Dianne learning about the construction business, Sherri?"

She laughed. A contagious laugh you wanted to join in with. "I don't think so. I should pay her as a labourer though. She's been lugging boxes this morning and helping me get set up. This should have been done last night, but..."

Dianne's grimace told me what I already knew about her affinity for physical labour - she was not impressed. "Labourer? Somehow, no. Call this a one-off to help a friend."

"Whatever you'd like to call it, Dianne, I'm indebted to you for your help this morning. You are hereby released from any further activities, and I'm ready to get down to business. Nice to meet you, Alysha. Hope our paths cross again."

"I'm sure they will. So, you don't mind if I take Dianne away for a bit?"

Sherri chuckled. "I've taken up enough of her time. Besides," she lowered her voice a notch and leaned her head towards people standing off to one side, "it appears there's some interest in Brodan Construction."

We said goodbye to Sherri, her attention at once taken up with a young couple, brochures in hand.

Dianne headed in the direction of her favourite hangout. "Let's find some seating in the Tavern. Not much room near the cafe. I'm sure Cassie can serve us coffee although I've probably had enough today."

Cassie must have overheard the coffee comment as we approached because she edged over to us ready with coffee before we'd even sat down. "Are you enjoying yourselves? It's so busy and I want to get to the Ferris wheel tonight. That's my favourite ride."

You'd never know Cassie had been in a life-threatening situation such a short time ago. It all rolled off her with little to no effort. Frustrating for Jan and me, but that was Cassie.

Dianne sighed. "My Ferris wheel days are done." She held up a hand. "And, sorry I changed my mind - no coffee. I've had enough. Just a glass of water for me. Lots of ice. Please."

"Same for me, Cassie." I glanced over at Jan doing a brisk trade as the empty shelves behind her attested to. I made a few random comments about fairgoers when Dianne interrupted me.

"Okay, Alysha, enough talking about everyone else. You've piqued my curiosity - what's on your mind about Bennett?"

"Let's get our water first." I took the opportunity—stalling more like—to look around as I waited on Cassie's return. Even when two plastic cups, filled with ice and water, arrived, I didn't speak. No need for our resident gossip to hear what I intended to say to Dianne about Bennett.

My parched throat enjoyed the first swallow of icy water, and I looked up to see Dianne's eager face expecting who knows what from me. She grinned from ear to ear, ready to explode with questions.

"Right, spit it out. Or, let me guess. He's offered you a partnership. Am I right, am I right?"

A partnership? Where on earth did she get that idea from? "No Dianne. For the record, I don't want to be in a partnership with Bennett. My goal is to have my own brokerage. Anyway, that's not what I want to discuss with you." I took a moment to compose my thoughts. I didn't want my words to contradict my claims of not spreading gossip. "It's Bennett - he's acting weird, and I feel uncomfortable around him. He arrived, late, this morning. He's always punctual or at least he would let me know if he's held up. Talked a mile a minute about how well I'm doing. Sounds like I'm the best thing since sliced bread."

"Well, that's a good thing, isn't it?"

"Not really. He's professional and these comments are a little out of character. I put it down to his breakup with Nina." I gulped down the rest of my water. "Is that the time? I need to get back to spell Bennett. Hope he's more himself by now."

***

Dianne

I was a little disappointed. Alysha had hinted at something substantial to tell me. Maybe she changed her mind and didn't feel like finger-pointing when it came to Nina and Bennett. I'd say old Bennett might just be suffering the consequences of being caught and he was the one who felt uncomfortable around Alysha. Too frigging bad.

And Nina? Wow, was she hot under the collar, or scarf, today! I didn't blame her for disliking the location of her booth. But she had to remember she was a last-minute participant, so had no basis to complain about being outside the busy, and noisy, public washroom and across from the livestock pens. Being irate with Bennett didn't help and I seriously doubted whether she'd last for the whole weekend of the Fair.

I'd seen a couple of women ramble by holding copies of one of her books, so she was making some sales. That should help. I deliberated whether we should stop by and offer moral support.

"On our way back, we should go by Nina's booth. I don't think she's a happy camper right now."

Alysha snorted. "You think? I'm not unsympathetic to her romance status but come on. She's a grown woman and is acting like a spoiled teenager." She narrowed her eyes at me. "Tell me I've behaved better over my break-up?"

"Like comparing oranges and apples. Listen when it comes to Nina, I think she jumped way too fast when Bennett crooked his finger at her. Better to find out now he's a rotten bastard, in the relationship department, than down the road."

"I suppose." She stood. "Thanks for hearing me out. But I need to get back now and give him a break. We could grab a hamburger later on my lunch break – around one o'clock?"

"Sounds like a plan. For now, I'll head over to the grandstand and take in the horse jumping event."

We were about to go our separate ways when two police cars pulled up. I don't know if Dubois wanted to showcase his driving skills, but the amount of dust he kicked up when he hit the brakes gave me, and a lot of others, a coughing fit.

The Grant's Crossing Police Department manned a tiny community outreach booth inside so maybe this was part of the presentation, although four officers in addition to the constable manning the display inside seemed like overkill.

Something in their bearing tickled my radar. "Forget the horses, Alysha, let's see where they're headed."

Dubois and his partner, Truman, headed inside. The other two branched out on either side of the building. Covering exits? Whatever their destination, they were garnering attention.

Jan spied them as Dubois and Truman strode by. They kept moving toward the other end of the barn. Stopping when they came to Bennett Howes' Real Estate display.

I glanced at Alysha, who now looked in Bennett's direction with her eyes wide open. "What's going on?"

We pushed our way through the crowd which had come to a standstill, voices hushed. Well, not all voices. As it grew quieter where we stood, Nina's voice rose above the crowd as she worked to entice buyers to her stall. She might be a best-selling author, but her sales pitch could do with some work. And then she must have caught on to where all the attention focused.

The three of us collided together as DC Steven Dubois stood in front of Bennett Howes. Who, I should mention, had turned ghastly pale, business cards dropping from his hands faster than autumn leaves.

Canned music from the midway outside lent to a surreal scene, as all activity around us had ceased. Alysha made a move to step toward Bennett, but I grabbed her arm and held her in check.

A small gasp came up from the crowd as Dubois unhooked his hand cuffs and moved closer to Bennett. Like watching a train wreck, I knew what was coming. Nina must have, too. She tensed beside me, but for once words escaped her.

"Bennett Howes. I'm here to arrest you on suspicion of the murder of April Lancashire."

Faster than the speed of light the crowd erupted. "No!" or "Doesn't surprise me" mixed with the rush of raised cell phones to capture the moment.

Bennett closed his eyes and held out his wrists.

"Bennett. I'll call a lawyer. They've made a mistake!" Alysha called out uselessly to the retreating backs of her boss and the police. Then she leaned into me to me and whispered. "They have made a mistake, haven't they? This can't be true."

Nina finally found her voice but kept it low. "Come with me, both of you. Outside where we can talk."

I could only nod because my brain couldn't wrap itself around what I'd just seen. After suspecting Griffith, Brock, Kyle Foreman and even Jeff, had the police at last got the right person? They'd been wrong before.

We trekked out into the brilliant sunshine. The police cars had gone, but the gossip flowed all around us. Someone spotted Alysha. "Hey. You work for Bennett. How did he do it?"

She stopped in her tracks. "If he did it, that's for the police to comment! Excuse us." Then she grabbed my arm and marched forward. I felt her trembling but gave her credit for holding her shit together.

By this time, Jan had caught up to us. "Are you all right, little one?"

Alysha's curls bounced wildly as she shook her head. No one said another word until we found a quiet spot at the far end of the parking lot.

No one wanted to start talking. Alysha wore a dazed expression, but I sensed, like the rest of us, she was trying to make sense of what happened. Jan looked on in concern, but it was Nina's somewhat smug expression that loosened my tongue. "Right, then, what do you know about all this, Nina?"

"It was me."

"You what?" My tolerance for long and drawn-out explanations had vanished.

Her intentional, and theatrical, gaze given to all three of us left me wondering whether she was angling for impact—and thinking of a writing opportunity—or maybe was genuinely aware of how anything she'd say could affect Alysha. I'd give her the benefit of the doubt on the latter.

"I spoke to the police yesterday about what I'd found at Bennett's home. At first, I was crazy mad he'd been cheating on me, but then I suspected he'd been cheating with—guess who—April Lancashire, while he'd been seeing me! Maybe I only thought of hurting him like he'd hurt me…"

We held our breath. What the hell was she going to say?

"…but then I realized I might have been sleeping with a murderer. And I don't know what upset me more!"

"What did you find, Nina?" Alysha's voice may have been calm, but I knew she didn't want any details sugar coated.

"Bennett's diary, you know those daily agenda things. And a receipt for a stay at one of the best hotels in Toronto. The weekend he told me we couldn't see each other because he was at a real estate conference in Windsor. The diary showed the initials AL with a reminder to buy wine/bring bracelet and the receipt was attached to a brochure for a romantic couple's weekend."

Whoa! I turned my attention to Alysha, who asked, "What was the date, Nina?"

When Nina told her, she pursed her lips and focused on people moving about in the distance. Her wheels were spinning, and after a moment she spoke. "Right, I remember that weekend. Bennett told me he'd be away for those days hunting antiques for his home office."

"Men!" was all I could manage to say.

Jan moved closer to Nina. "For what it's worth. I am sorry." She stopped as if a thought had taken root. "If he is guilty of this murder, you may have made a lucky escape. Listen, ladies. I suggest we keep what we've talked about to ourselves. And I foresee police contact with you, Alysha, as well as Nina, before you know it."

"You're probably right, Jan." Alysha took charge. "So, for now, if we can, we should get back to our responsibilities for the rest of the fair. In light of what's happened, I should close up my area."

"A smart decision," said Jan. "It will only become the centre of attention and that's not what this weekend is about. Dianne, will you help her? I need to get back and Nina has her books." Then she made an observation, which I was about to comment on as well.

"And for goodness sake, not a word to Cassie. She must have left the fairgrounds, or she'd have found us by now!"

Nina laughed. "You gals are something else. I'll miss you. But I agree with Jan. Zipped lips and all that. I won't even tell Hemingway!"

We knew there'd be questions from Rose and Minnie if no one else. But we had time, I hoped, to prepare. Most of the questions would be for Alysha - as long as we kept Nina's involvement out of it. I looked at Alysha as we walked back to the exhibition building. For all intents and purposes, I believe if anyone saw her with us, we'd only taken a lunch break and were heading back to our posts.

But I couldn't wait until the three of us could have a decent talk before the day ended. This was one fair that wouldn't be forgotten in a hurry.

I stayed with Alysha as Jan and Nina took off in different directions. "I'll give you a hand to close your display. I guess you'll need to do something about the office as well?"

"Thanks. Yes. And I promised to get a lawyer for Bennett – he probably has one on file in the office. Oh, I just can't believe this! If he's guilty..."

"A lot of mixed emotions, right?"

"I can't even begin to sort through them. And is it bad of me to question what will happen to his business?"

"Not bad, practical. But nothing that can't wait until we know the outcome. Until then, I'm sure you'll be up to the task. There's another agent there as well, though?"

"You're right. Oh, my God. Look at the gawkers!"

True enough; Bennett Howes' display had a disproportionate number of interested people milling about. As we moved closer, I channelled Jan. "Nothing to see here folks. The show is over. Move along."

There wasn't much to pack up and we were soon done. Nothing left to show the display had ever advertised Bennett Howes' Real Estate. Alysha did well ignoring those persistent enough to remain. At least until her cell phone rang. She took the call, disconnected, and turned to me.

"Here we go again. Dianne, will you come with me to the police station?"

CHAPTER TWENTY-EIGHT

Alysha

The day had morphed into a nightmare – how would it end? Now my boss has been charged with the murder of April Lancashire. At least I was glad I hadn't said anything about Griffith to Dianne. It was a moot point now.

I was grateful for Dianne's company, but, if I never saw the inside of the Grant's Crossing police department again it would be too soon.

Every room in the tiny station was cramped. The cubicle Dubois crammed us into made me think a phone booth would be preferable, at least it would have windows! Dubois, playing messenger for Bennet, only had a brief discussion with us concerning Bennett—still the businessman—wanted to ensure I'd be supportive of his long-time agent, Ernie, for the foreseeable future. He and I were to split Bennett's client list between us. But it was to me he'd refer to for anything dealing with his lawyer and representation. Would I be his liaison?

I didn't know what to think. Business wise I was fine with the office arrangement, but to have any contact with a murderer - even if it was remotely through a lawyer? I turned to Dianne. "What do you think I should do about the liaison part?"

She raised her eyebrows. "Kiddo, that's a tough call. You have my vote of confidence you'll find the right balance." She paused. "And, if by some miracle, Bennett Howes isn't locked up, you'll be glad you didn't cut all the ties with him."

"Okay, then. Yes, detective, you can tell Bennett I'll talk with his lawyer, and I'll do my best where the office is concerned."

Dubois scribbled on the notepad in front of him and then handed over a slip of paper with a more detailed note on contact information for the lawyer. That's it then, ladies. Thank you for coming."

"That's it? Has he confessed?" Had they dragged me down here for this?

Dubois just smiled and laid a finger beside his nose. "Ms. Grant - Alysha - you should know better than to ask."

Seeing as we were here, I had another question to be answered. "And Griffith Sharples, what about him. He'd made threats to April, or at least said he did. We heard him make claim she'd be sorry, or something? Didn't we, Dianne?"

"He has been cleared of murder charges but must answer for what he did to Cassie, er, Ms. DeSouza. Those threats he claims against April Lancashire? Overblown and wishful thinking on his part. Now, ladies, if you'll excuse me."

Dianne and I left the police station, got in my car, and headed back to Leven Lodge My hands clenched the steering wheel. "Do they have the right man this time, Dianne?"

"After all the wrong suspects, and with no plea of innocence from Howes, I'd say so. Sorry, Alysha. This must be a real blow for you."

We drove up the drive and I parked in my spot, but I needed to talk more before we left the car. "It's so hard to believe. I admire the man and he's such a prominent figure in the community. I thought I was a better judge of character."

"Don't berate yourself. Seems like you weren't the only one he fooled. And things happen in the heat of passion. That might be his defence, but we'll have to wait for all the why's and where's before we jump to conclusions."

"Time will tell. It's a lot to take in. Thanks for coming with me, I'll take you back later to get your car if that's all right?"

"No worries. You might want to give Jan a call and let her know we're home now."

"Good idea. She'll need to know I won't be coming back, and she's likely anxious for an update as well. She and Cassie are supposed to stay there until the booths close, but she might want to come home sooner."

***

Turned out I drove Dianne back to the fairgrounds for her car sooner than I planned. A call from Ernie Peak at the office had me going back into town and I dropped her off. Poor guy was understandably upset, same as Christine, but after we talked and made tentative plans, they both relaxed. We contacted a few clients and then put the Closed sign in the window.

And when I contacted Jan, she had promised to be home earlier than the 9:00 p.m. closing. "Most of my pies have sold anyway. I might be there around supper time but go ahead and eat whenever you're hungry."

By the time I got back to the Lodge, the sun had set, leaving an orange glow in the western sky, and I'd cultivated a brute of a headache. Dianne met me at the front door, but I put a hand up. "I need to close my eyes for about half an hour. By then Jan should be home."

"Go lie down, kiddo. This has been a wicked day. Nina came back and has been rummaging around in her room. Best to stay out of her way I'd say." She looked at her watch. "Think you'll want something to eat?"

I nodded; the effort sent a wave of throbbing pressure to my head. "I'll come downstairs in an hour. Meet you in the kitchen."

***

About ninety minutes later, I joined Dianne in the kitchen. The headache had subsided but hadn't vacated completely. Hunger pangs were a positive sign, I thought.

Dianne had set a couple of places at the large kitchen table, and I heard the microwave humming. Jan's efficiency at preparing food for the home paid off.

After the first bite of a hearty chicken casserole, my appetite kicked in. Dianne was making short work of hers as well. We hadn't talked much; the food was too delicious!

Headlights reflected in the kitchen window caught my attention. "Jan's home." I said.

The back door opened. "Oh, that smells good. I hope you've left me some because I am famished and done in. Selling pies is exhausting, and hungry work."

While she went to freshen up, we set out a place for her. "Looks like Cassie didn't come back with her."

Dianne snickered. "For small mercies we should be extremely thankful."

Jan returned and sat at the chair I pulled out for her, and I began to dish out a healthy serving of casserole. "Ah, this is perfect, little one. Thank you." A pot of fresh tea stood ready.

As Jan tackled her main course, Dianne tilted her head toward a pie under its glass cover. Jan chuckled. "Go ahead, but make it three pieces, please. And now while I eat, fill me in on the latest. Anything more from Steven Dubois? He's not like Dax though. Keeps things close to himself."

"Well to be fair, Jan, Dax probably gave you more info at times than he should have, because you're his aunt." Dianne teased, but I agreed with her. We probably would have more details if Dax were here. I briefly pondered how he was, and then just as quickly pushed the thought away.

The furnace rumbled in the basement below my feet, reminding me cooler nights were normal now. The cold air from the opening front door had likely triggered the furnace setting. We heard laughter. Sounded as if Frank had returned with his harem. Jan stood. "I'll just check and see if anyone is hungry."

She came back a moment later. "They've all eaten at the fair. Frank has dropped them off and is going home after he checks on the alpacas. The ladies are all headed to their rooms, dead on their feet."

The house quietened around us, and we sat back. Well fed, but questions were on Jan's mind. "So, it's not likely anyone will forget the events this morning in a hurry. Do we know, or believe it's true? That Bennett Howes killed April Lancashire? What a spectacle!"

I didn't have much more to add to what we already knew. "I may learn more after I talk with Bennett's lawyer, but for now I guess we believe it's true. Nina certainly believes it."

"Are you telling me what Nina told us is true? He was seeing April as well as Nina?" Jan rose from her seat and turned to face us. "I've known him for years and would never have thought him capable of such... of such callousness. He certainly fooled a lot of people, not just Nina."

She was unsettled. Her earlier fatigue replaced by indignation. "Part of me would like to put the blame on Nina. I knew that woman was going to cause a stir the moment I laid eyes on her. She and her dog have been nothing but trouble. But I can't. The fault lies with Bennett."

"Jan, please sit down. It's not worth getting this worked up over. She's upstairs now as far as I know, and by this time next week, will be history - once the police have no further interest in what she has to say." My headache had fired up again, sapping my energy levels.

She sighed. "I'm sorry. You're right, she's not worth the energy." She sat down and composed herself. "Is there more tea, Dianne?"

While Dianne obliged, Jan wanted to know why Dubois had wanted to see me at the station, so I explained Bennett's requests.

"C'mon, Jan," teased Dianne, "don't you know Dax isn't the only Grant's Crossing officer sweet on Alysha."

I had no patience for where this might lead. "Change the subject, Dianne. It's not funny."

And then Jan put a finger to her lips. "Shh!" as her eyes went to the dining room doorway.

Two inquisitive, but concerned faces peeked in at us. The Patels.

Jan stood and moved over to them. "Have you just come home? There's plenty of food to eat if you're looking for supper."

Bachan smiled. "Oh, please to not worry, dear Jan. We are well fed. We heard the chatting and chitting and wanted to make sure everyone is home so safe and sound by now. That is all."

Sasitha smiled. "My poor husband suffers so. No beer on draught for him this evening, but only bottled." Her laugh infected all of us and we couldn't help but smile.

Then her smile left, replaced by a frown. "We did hear of a big upsetting time near you, Alysha. We had been in the outside but saw the police come and then Nina and all of you were coming outside, looking oh so worried. It was not news of something bad, I hope?"

I came over and stood by Jan. "You are both so sweet. Please don't worry. Yes, it was bad news. The man I work for, Bennett Howes, has been arrested for the murder of April Lancashire. But we are all fine. I only hope it didn't dampen your enjoyment of the Fall Fair?"

Sasitha handed me a box. "No, no. Not at all. But that is most terrible news for you. We are both very sorry."

I couldn't resist giving her a quick hug. "Thank you."

Then she bounced right back with a smile big enough to match an excited child at Christmas. "Did you try the Ferris wheel, Alysha? That is my most favourite of rides to go on. So much fun I am telling you. And when it is stopping at the top there is so much to see!" She tapped the box. "Please. Take this. Those are a few treats for tomorrow's dinner we wanted to share. And now we will leave you to your evening, but only to must say we so enjoy living here. Good night."

Sasitha's words couldn't have come at a better time and soothed me. "And we enjoy having you both here, as well. Good night."

Jan took the box from me, peeked inside, and smiled. "Oh yes, these squares will be enjoyed at day's end tomorrow." She looked at Dianne and me. "I suggest we take the same advice and call it a night. It's another early start tomorrow. But maybe not for you, Alysha?"

I shrugged. "Truthfully, I haven't thought that far ahead. But for me and my headache, I'm ready to say goodnight."

And so, we did.

***

Dianne

"I'm going to miss you so much," Lily's lip quivered as she stroked Hemingway sitting on her lap.

Rose sighed in exasperation. "By all means, Lily, comfort the dog. The rest of us can do all the work for our special lunch."

Hemingway snarled and I bit the inside of my cheek. Really, Rose. What work? The noon-day meal was being catered, and Jan had set the table. But I guess fussing over the table centrepiece could be considered work in her view.

It had been a busy morning. The Fair had ended last night, and Halloween was tonight. Right now, the main event was Nina's promised lunch as her way of saying thanks and farewell. She planned to leave before dark.

We'd squeezed in more chairs so Frank and Cory could join us for the occasion, as well as Cassie.

"I'll put this in the trunk," Cory called out to Nina as he took another piece of luggage out to her car.

Once lunch finished, our fractious temporary house guest would be leaving, with her muse, Hemingway.

Nina flounced into the dining room. Oh my god. She'd frosted the tips of her hair pumpkin-orange to match the black and orange yoga pants. A sequined black tunic top, festooned with skulls and witches' hats was over the top, even for her.

"The room's looking good, chickees. Food should be here at noon. Oh, and there's my snuggums. Time for a walk. One last stroll." She reached down to take Hemingway from Lily's lap and for a moment I thought Lily wouldn't relinquish him.

I wasn't needed so went upstairs and knocked on Alysha's door.

She seemed glad of the diversion. I could see a pile of paperwork behind her. "If you're busy I'll see you later."

"No, come on in. I have coffee made?" She didn't expect an answer and pulled a clean mug down for me.

"Nina's almost packed up," I said as I took the hot coffee from her.

"The elevator's been getting a workout this morning, I bet."

"Oh, and you should see Lily and that dog. She's not happy to be losing him."

"Who'd have thought she'd form an attachment."

I looked over the rim of my coffee mug to assess my friend. Small talk wasn't her thing, but she made the effort this morning. "So, how are you?" Likely seeing Jeff and Gillian returning the alpacas first thing hadn't helped.

She put her mug down. "I'm not sure how I should be. I had an email from Bennett's lawyer this morning confirming there'll be no trial because the police have accepted his confession." She shook her head. "I still can't believe it! The lawyer's not saying much. But from what I can piece together in addition to what Nina told us, he went to see April Lancashire at the theatre, not long after the scene with Brock. April was probably already in a bad temper and then confronted Bennett about his affair with Nina."

I couldn't help but shudder. "I don't understand how she found out?"

Alysha looked at me as if I were that dense. "If Nina figured it out, I'm sure April did as well."

"Right. Anything else?"

"Only Bennett and the police, I guess, know exactly what happened, but I imagine it was a heated confrontation. She probably gave him an ultimatum. And if I know Bennett at all, he's not one to be backed into a corner." I paused. "I gather he cooled down enough after killing her to try and cover her body with sheets of plywood. He'd been wearing his hallmark leather gloves at the time..."

"I can fill in the blanks. That's why only Jeff's fingerprints were found. So, no trial, just a sentencing?"

"Yep. Next week, the lawyer said. I don't think I'll go."

I agreed with her. "And you've got things sorted at the office?"

She uttered a harsh laugh and pointed to the mess on the table. "That's what I'm doing now. Ernie is understandably shaken. He's worked with Bennett for years. He's handed all the responsibilities over to me and wants me to be in charge. Which Christine seems happy with as well. So, there are legalities involved, but not today."

I matched the forced tone of optimism in her voice. "Exactly. Today is about Leven Lodge. Minnie's strutting around with her second-place ribbon on her sweater and Jan can't stop smiling over winning two first-place ribbons with her pies."

"And our celebratory lunch. Nina's big blowout. She's ecstatic there'll be no trial and told me the police have all they need from her so she's free to leave Grant's Crossing."

I laughed. "The police are probably relieved not to have to deal with her!"

"Oh, here's one thing Jan and I have discussed, and we'll tell the others after Nina's left, but we're going to offer Frank her room, with the provision he continues helping out here, as much as he's able. And to assist with Minnie."

"What a brilliant idea..." Before I could say more Jan's voice came over the intercom.

"Alysha. The food has arrived. Time for lunch."

***

Laughter, food, and friends. We had an abundance of all and even after all the delicious morsels had been consumed, no one was in a hurry to leave. Philip's book lay unopened.

"Are you sure you need to leave us today, Nina?" asked Lily. "Aren't there more notes you need for your book on Rose and me?"

Nina stood. "Sorry, Lily, but the road calls and I'd like to be on my way before dark. Besides, I know how to contact you if need be." She turned to Cory. "Everything is in the car now, young man?"

"Yes, ma'am."

"Oh, no... do not call me ma'am!"

More laughter and I hoped Cory saw the teasing as a sign of affection.

"I should stay and help with the clean-up..."

"But you won't," finished Jan, not unkindly. "Nina, we've had our moments during your stay, but I will be the first to admit you did bring some *enthusiasm* to the lodge." She paused. "I might regret this, but the door to Leven Lodge will always be open to you."

Nina made a sweeping curtesy. "Thank you. All of you. You made me feel at home and I've enjoyed getting to know each of you."

The table erupted with applause, and Hemingway's yips joined the chorus. That Jan had allowed the dog to sit at Nina's feet told me her offer of an open door was genuine. Or maybe the wine had me feeling sentimental.

A few minutes later, we stood en masse on the veranda and waved as Nina and her constant companion drove off down the driveway.

Alysha took me aside. "Still want to join me for a pizza this evening to avoid the trick or treaters? I thought I'd ask Jan as well. The others are more than capable of handing out treats."

"Absolutely!"

CHAPTER TWENTY-NINE

Alysha

Halloween - not my favourite night of the year. I preferred to leave the candy-seeking ghosts and goblins for someone else to greet. Last year it had been Jeff and I cocooned in our apartment to wait out the tide of trick or treaters. Tonight, Jan and Dianne joined me, and we relaxed as we waited on a pizza delivery.

I'd asked Frank to hang out with Minnie, and the twins, who were excited about the children coming for their treats. Cory was on hand to ensure the candy didn't run out, cell phone at the ready for picture taking. The pumpkins were lit on the veranda and the driveway had orange and white fairy lights to mark the way. White muslin had been draped from lower tree branches to depict ghosts drifting with the breeze. I didn't offer an opinion. Was it too soon to ask about Christmas decorations?

We'd just started into a discussion about our favourite subject, Nina, when Cory came bounding up the stairs.

"Pizza delivery."

Jan jumped up to accept the delivery and told our latest member of the Leven Lodge family where she'd hidden extra candies if they were needed.

"I'm glad you told me. Minnie is being awfully generous with her handouts!"

"Off you go then. If there's any problems, you know where we are."

Cory turned and darted off to the top of the stairs as Dianne looked on benevolently. She couldn't be prouder of him if she'd given birth. I felt contented the fates had smiled on them both to bring them together.

Jan commented on his height. "I believe that boy might have the proverbial hollow leg judging by the food I've seen him consume here. If he puts on weight once he stops growing, he could be a giant."

"A gentle giant at that," said Dianne, almost to herself. And then in a louder voice, "He's going to be fine. Doing well in school and he's not afraid of hard work."

Jan and I waited for her to continue, but she changed the topic.

"Now where were we? Oh yes, Nina. I must say she certainly stirred things up around here. Her stay probably didn't have the outcome she'd anticipated. Wouldn't surprise me, though, if she manages to write about it! I might have enjoyed her personality more than others," she winked at Jan, "but have to agree she's not a good fit for Leven Lodge."

While Dianne had been speaking, I dished out the tantalizing pizza for us. We mulled over the past few months Nina had spent here, and lessons we'd all learned.

Between bites, I had my say. "I agree totally and in future I'll take more care about who can move here. And pets. It's not fair to the others although Lily would disagree. We have enough with the farm animals."

Dianne wagged a finger at me. "Never say never, my friend."

Jan tucked into another slice of pizza. "Hmm, we must have this again. But only when Cassie's not around in case she thinks her job is threatened."

I giggled a bit at the observation. "She didn't mind taking part in Nina's lunch today, did she?"

"True, little one. After the weekend we've just come through, I know I was happy not to be thinking about what everyone would eat today. Cassie is no different." She wiped her hands after finishing her slice, then looked at Dianne and me. "I'll be honest and say Nina and Hemingway were a handful but now that Frank has agreed to move into her room and help with Minnie it's best for everyone.

Dianne's smile didn't hide her mischievous tone. "Having another man at the table for mealtimes will be nice. I'm sure Bachan will appreciate a man's point of view amongst all the female chatter. Maybe they could sit together."

After the pizza boxes were cleared away, we settled with a pot of tea. Jan and Dianne had to be as tired of the drama of the last few days as I was, because we were not our usual vocal selves. Apart from the fact we were stuffed. Catered lunch at Nina's leaving party and now pizza!

But Dianne never fails to ask the questions I don't feel like answering. "So, Alysha, what's happening with Bennett's office and his clients? Can you see yourself running the business without him? He had a big name in town so what about his clients, and all the committees he sat on?"

I lay back on the sofa cushions and took a deep breath before answering her. "Dianne, give me a break. This has only just happened and it's a lot to take in. I'll do the best I can with Ernie and Christine's help. Bennett is definitely out of the picture and there are a lot of things to settle. I'll probably be paying a visit to Bryce Lockhart for legal advice next week. But right now, I don't want to think about it!"

Jan sat beside me and gave me a hug. "I don't want you worrying about anything here at the lodge, little one. We are all hale and hearty right now, so let's not borrow trouble. The alpacas are doing fine. Philip and Cory manage them well with help from Frank. We'll deal with any problems if they arise."

She pulled back from me and glanced at Dianne. "Maybe we should put Dianne on the payroll. Not sure what, or who, we could put her in charge of though. But I always need extra help in the garden. Are you ready to dig up turnips and potatoes, Dianne?"

Jan had lightened the mood and we laughed - visions of Dianne with a shovel and mud under her manicured nails ran through my head.

"Er, no, thank you all the same for the wonderful offer. Manual labour isn't part of my genetic heritage, but I'll speak to Cory and see if he wants extra hours."

I wandered over to the windows overlooking the driveway. Not much moonlight to penetrate the inky darkness. From what I could see, there were no more costumed visitors with plastic pumpkins paying a visit. Another Halloween I managed to avoid.

I relaxed even more. Apart from Halloween, I loved my life here in Grant's Crossing and the people who lived at my family's homestead. Staff who have become friends to help me run the lodge - my family legacy - while I stretch my wings with a career away from the home. Even a fleeting thought of my single life without Jeff didn't have as much sting. I'd outgrown the betrayal and was moving on.

I turned back from the window to see Dianne closing her eyes. Jan fussed in my small kitchen, sorting the garbage to take down. Always on duty. How grateful I am for her friendship.

I inclined my head in Dianne's direction. "We might be keeping her up."

"That will never do." Jan finished her tidying up and moved over to Dianne. "Wakey, wakey. I think the past few days have caught up and we all need to say goodnight."

Before Dianne could respond, the intercom came to life. Frank wasn't familiar with how it worked, and it took a couple of tries before he could spit out a message.

"Jan? This is Frank. Frank Adams, you know?"

Dianne put her fingers to her lips to squash a giggle.

"Yes, Frank. Go ahead. Do you need me to come down?"

"If you would, please. Your nephew, Dakotah, is here."

My world changed in a heartbeat.

DID YOU KNOW?

Jamie Tremain is not one person, but two! Pam Blance and Liz Lindsay are Jamie Tremain.

In the summer of 2007 Pam and Liz began their writing journey as Jamie Tremain when it was discovered they shared a love of reading – and writing!

Currently Jamie Tremain has two series. The Dorothy Dennehy Mystery Series and The Grant's Crossing series.

Even before their first book in The Dorothy Dennehy Mystery Series was published, they had been actively building their brand. One of their fortes was, and still is, interviews on their blog with other authors, and readers. Networking with the supportive writing community continues to be a priority.

A recent "Author Survival Network" private group was established on Facebook to offer fellow authors a place to meet, share experiences and offer encouragement to each other.

Jamie Tremain belongs to Crime Writers of Canada, International Thriller Writers, and are proud to be part of the Genre5 Writers group in Guelph, Ontario.

Liz Pam

You can learn more at www.jamietremain.ca[1] , https://www.facebook.com/jamietremainwrites

Or email us at jamietremainJT@yahoo.com

Books by Jamie Tremain
THE DOROTHY DENNEHY MYSTERY SERIES

- The Silk Shroud
- Lightning Strike
- Beholden to None

THE GRANT'S CROSSING SERIES

- Death on the Alder
- Resort to Murder
- Acting Off-Script

Books in each series are best read in order, and are available online at Amazon, Google Play, Kobo, Apple Books, etc.

Don't miss out!

Visit the website below and you can sign up to receive emails whenever Jamie Tremain publishes a new book. There's no charge and no obligation.

https://books2read.com/r/B-A-VAAO-GAQAC

BOOKS 2 READ

Connecting independent readers to independent writers.